# DRAGONSOUL
## THE NEW GENERATION

Rosie
Another one for the pile!! Hope you feel better soon. :)
x

Story written by

S. L. Colkin

First independently published through Amazon Kindle in 2020.

All characters and events in this book are fictional. Any similarity to real persons, living or dead, is coincidental and not intended by the author.



The CIP catalogue record for this book is available from the British Library

ISBN 978-1-9163756-0-4

To Milli & Daisy

# Acknowledgement Page

This book would not have been possible without the encouragement from my family and friends who have supported me in the real world and in this one.

I would like to thank Pixel Clan, from 99designs.co.uk, for turning my rambling ideas into the amazing book cover design and putting up with many '*could we try…*'moments. A big thank you to Chris Cartwright for proofreading my book and going above and beyond to spot my unusual use of capital letters. And finally, to the awesome group of people who took the time to read my book, give me feedback and push me to take the leap.

# Chapters

# Prologue

*Time past:*

*Time had come full circle in the world of men. From myths and legends, gods and worship, science and understanding to now, a time for magic and chaos. This new era in its infancy: a growing entity yet to be fully realised. The first signs of change happened when dragons flew the skies once more.*

*Their time of hiding, in the depths of the land, was coming to an end, but so was their life. No longer could their wings support their massive bodies through the sky gracefully nor could their breath bring life to fire. Their scales were dull, their wings drooping and the effort to fly but a short distance a sad demonstration of their glory days. They had slumbered for an age, gaining wisdom, and as their final breaths of life drew ever closer, they came to man with an offer. The dragonkin of the world understood that magic would be brought into the world once more, and they knew what would be unleashed. It was the ultimate drive that pushed them to make their final stand - to act on the thoughts of a millennia.*

---

Time to come:

'The balance. The balance! That's all those wilders talk about. Do they even know what the balance is?' A harsh voice clips the end of the sentence short as the Governess's lips close into a tight line. The sharpness of spiked heels walking across the sparse office floor becomes the only noise as Prudence walks to stand in front of the data displays before her. 'It's written on every media feed as the words infect our society, and those backwards folks don't even understand the meaning. Do you? What about you?' Spiked hair hardly moves as the Governess turns to face the few other individuals in the room as she snaps out her question. 'What about you?' She points a finger at a young girl stood beside a couple dressed for business. Suddenly sparks fly, and the young girl drops to the floor lifeless.

Disregarding the young girl, the Governess looks down to the hand she pointed with. Her eyes are wide and her fake eyelashes flutter. Transfixed, she looks at her hand. There is no outward sign, but it feels to her like electricity is cracking around her fingers, dancing from tip to palm.

The silhouette holds for a moment before Prudence snaps her fingers closed and a sneer spreads across her features. 'The time is approaching - I can feel it. Now you two know what you need to do. Go!' Her hand raises again to point her finger at the remaining couple. They flinch but nothing happens. Seeing this as a sign they should leave, they scurry away from the office. Prudence tries a few more times to entice the current back to her fingers, but nothing happens. 'Patience, Prudence' She mumbles to herself before turning to return to her stark desk.

# Chapter 1

# Royals Meet

At the time of the first ripples of the awakening, the world was divided. Technology had led cities to be metropolises of high-speed connections, holographic sales, electric cars and tall buildings slicing into the horizon. In-between these sprawling skyscrapers were bands of green woodland, fields, farmland and villages made up of haphazard houses, rivers and lakes a place which is a haven for all nature. During the 21st Century the human population had become divided in their thinking, which had caused these extremes in living environments. People had real concerns about the sustainability of the earth and had begun to consider eco living, but at the same time technology and the sciences were going from strength to strength. From now, being 2167, you could trace the divide back as far as 2017 when governments argued over global warming, fossil fuels, the age of the human population and many more topics which seemed to divide people's thinking. Nobody could know how the future would look as this division became different paths.

Coming forward to the present day, at birth you are tagged, chipped, identified and your genes scanned to decide if you are a best suited as a city dweller or a land lover. Once decided, your education, dress style and whole life is guided towards where you would end up. Most family bloodlines stay in the hold or wild of their founders as their way of life guided the next generations, but, occasionally, people would choose a different route. In reality, this social divide is all a myth; one side cannot live without the other: the farm and nature providing the antidote to the city along with all the products needed to feed the metallic holds while the city provided the medicines and the products to keep the natural wilds sustainable. The two eco-systems have evolved into a symbiotic relationship that support each other, and a fine balance between the holds and surrounding wilds creates a working sustainability. It seems strange that the natural wilds, with their feeling of medieval living, could ever compare to the decadence of the metallic holds, but it is a fact that the two coexist! On rare occasions people from either world might visit the other, but they always go home.

The world has evolved and changed greatly, with countries' borders moving and continents colliding. Since the United Kingdom cut all ties with its neighbours during the years after 2019, it had slowly become a self-sufficient forgotten island, and this is where our story is set.

For this story, the natural wilds of Warwick are the focal point. Warwick was one of those cities that never made it as a metallic marker. Perhaps because Coventry & Birmingham took that role from it or perhaps because the castle was so entrenched in history that nobody wished to lose it, but Warwick became one of the largest natural wilds, governed from the very castle that had spent many years being a tourist attraction, and was now the home of the DragonWalker Council and all the advisers for the wilds. Some of the other cities to fall to the wilds include Exeter, Truro, Leeds (Manchester and the steel works of Sheffield being too strong), Glasgow and Cardiff. The fallen cities held echoes of the past in their local architecture or broken-down roads and streets, but the habitat had taken hold and was far stronger than the historic manmade buildings.

Sitting in a small library room in Warwick Castle were John and Eric: identical twin boys approaching their 18$^{th}$ birthday. Their strawberry blond hair, pale complexion and slate grey eyes gave them a striking look when matched with their trim physique. The only differences between them were the style in which their hair was cut, their choice of clothes and the look in their eyes. John, the older of the two by only a few hours, was the first born and heir to the throne. He knew responsibility would fall to him and had studied accordingly. He was calm, focused, pleasant yet quietly reserved. People treated him respectfully and he helped his family to support the land they ruled. Eric on the other hand, though still respected by the people, made those around him cautious as they knew that his personality had spikes of anger; he was reckless at times and a lot more inclined to act with his fists than remain quiet. Eric knew his time on the throne would not come in the natural order so had not spent as much time in study and was a lot less reserved. In many ways the brothers were opposites, but they got on well and seemed to balance each other out. Their time was often split between study, supporting the people and following the athletic hobbies both enjoyed. The boys were supposed to be studying, but their minds kept drifting to more important things.

'Oh, come on John, we know this stuff already! When the DragonSoul Stone stands before us in the council of the DragonWalkers, the twelve chosen will receive a soul, thus making them the new generation of Walkers, heralding them as the new council members of the wilds and adviser to all the wild lands. Why do we have to learn more about this - we are part of the twelve.'

John shook his head at Eric and rolled his eyes, knowing it would fuel his brothers' anger.

'You know that we are also entrusted to guide and nurture the magic if it returns to the land; if it happens in our lifetime then we work with it and help guide the magic to a positive flow. If the magic doesn't return, we pass on the knowledge to the next generation in another 50 years. We were chosen because of our strong position within the wilds. Other cities will each send two representatives from their households, and they will have been trained with the skill to lead, support and nurture their people.'

Eric disagreed with this point and made it blatantly clear.

'John, you know as well as I do that the other Royal families heirs won't have been working on this as you have, but they will be there all the same, and who even knows if this old information is correct?' Eric sighed. 'I mean look, Glasgow is sending Simon and Liam; Exeter, Arron and Darryn; Leeds, Chris and Malinky; Truro, Tanya and Johan; and Cardiff, Zack and …' He faltered on the last person's name, leaving a pause for John to cut back in

'Jo. Yes, I know who they are sending, and you should be glad that the council agreed that Warwick could put us two forward. Our father said they were not sure how one of us would cope with the other changed so, but that doesn't mean they won't change their mind. There are others in our family line of age. Just work at your studies and don't do anything that could lose us our good fortune!!' The conversation at an end, both turned back to their books and the air turned still.

To keep the council strong and the natural wilds united it was agreed that each city would send two of their Royal children to stand before the DragonSoul Stone. Warwick was going to be the host city for the monumental moment of the DragonSoul Awakening, and preparations were happening all over the wild. All knew that the parade to take the prized possession to the castle would be a grand affair and would bring in visitors from across the land even from the metallic holds. This event had only happened once before, at a time when nobody remembered the dragons, yet all felt the feeling of awe in their wake.

Though the event was weeks away, the central wild began to swell in numbers as traders, tourists and supporters had started to fill its ragged streets. Houses originally created for a family of four now extended their walls with wood, old corrugated iron and twine of any size to hold six, seven, eight people. Families spread across the wilds were beginning to reform, unite and share stories and music. The feel in the town was steadily growing in momentum but everyone held themselves in check as they knew the event was still some time away.

The first Royals to enter Warwick came from the southern quarter and entered with no fanfare, no pomp at all. The horses they rode were stock shire horses, their coats glistening with a slight sweat from a long ride, their dappled colouring a contrast to the simple greys that the riders wore. The party carried the chosen Royals from Devon and Cornwall. It consisted of two Royals from each county, their heads of house who were their legal guardians while in Warwick, and two guide riders. The group made their way toward the majestic castle without stopping at any shops but chatting happily amongst themselves. Their accent was strong with a twang that nobody could fail to recognise. The conversation flowed to anyone who might be passing but people might only have understood one or two words. The main topic of the conversation seemed to the Metallic Holds of Plymouth and Bristol. The group had stopped within these holds to break up their journey and were happily discussing with amusement that the virtual world they had entered for an evening's entertainment seemed to be based on the wilds, but that they had not got the feel correct.

'They should just come out and experience it why plug in? Can't experience the breeze that way. Nothing like a sea breeze!' More chuckles as the conversation drifted on. 'And what about that synthesised music? Think they would like some old folk stuff? Hmmm?? They wouldn't know how to clap to a live performance anyhow!!'

Once they reached the entrance gates, now rusted with time but still looking ominous in their vastness, the group slowed to a stop and waited to be recognised and addressed. Following confirmation of title and reason for being at the castle gate, all dismounted. The guide riders took their leave to look after the horses while the guardians were asked to walk with their charges into the main hall. All were silent. John and Eric stood to the side of their father while he did the address, although they were keenly eyeing the four young Royals. First to be introduced were Arron and Darryn from Exeter. Arron was of stocky build but seemed to be rounded. His chest was more barrelled than chiselled, but he had a ready smile to match his lively blue eyes and curly mahogany hair. Darryn was the opposite: lean, greased hair, appearing to fold in on himself while his eyes seemed to focus ahead without really looking. The pair seemed good natured enough, but the Warwick twins weren't so sure of them. The second pair were from Truro and seemed to be much more interesting. Johan was the athletic type with broad shoulders, sculpted waist, sharp features and a sharp haircut to match. It was almost the same style as Eric's with the spikes seeming to go in all directions all on their own. The final Royal was Tanya. Both John and Eric were taken aback when they realised a female had been chosen, as it was thought that the DragonSoul required male to male bonds; but then, who was to say that female dragons didn't also give their souls for man? Tanya looked strong, standing tall, a well-rounded chest rising above a shapely figure. She was not as skinny as Darryn appeared nor rounded like Arron, but her body seemed to be in comfortable sync with itself. The four Royals had noticed the twins, but duty required them to pay attention to the ruler of the hosting wild, and just like the twins, they did not want to do anything that would jeopardise this opportunity.

*Time was drawing closer. The shell of the DragonSoul Stone had begun to ripple with the colours of the souls that would pass through it. It was not yet fully complete, but all around the vault could feel the life that flowed from around its edges. Nobody of this generation had seen the stone alive, only the lifeless golden orb that sat on its pedestal within the protection of stone and metal. The council felt it and knew their time was coming to an end, but still they rejoiced as the new generation was forming.*

The next group of Royals had come from the north and their entry had been as much of a parade as what was to come. The guide riders rode horses that looked fit to ride at ascot rather than the tracks from Glasgow & Leeds. Again, it seemed that wilds had teamed up for the long journey. John and Eric's father once again greeted the group and welcomed them to Warwick, his hands rising slightly to draw attention to the beauty of the castle. From Glasgow came Simon and Liam. They were obviously brothers but possibly a year apart in age. They had dark hair that flopped around their head in no particular style, their olive complexion matching their dark eyes. Both were average in height and stature.

Chris and Malinky from Leeds were a different matter. They, like the Exeter Royals, could not be more different.

Chris was tall, hair almost down to his hips with dark eyes that darted around taking everything in. Malinky was short, hair cropped close to his scalp though he too had eyes that seemed to be looking at everything at once. They communicated with a simple nod and then not another physical motion was made.

‘John, this means there is only Cardiff to arrive. We can then maybe finally stop all this non-committal stuff and begin our training. We might even get to go into the council chamber!’

‘Don’t be strange, you know that won’t happen in case anything goes wrong. You know you’re only able to enter that room if the souls are entwined’

‘Pfft, you know I’m not interested in that kind of stuff. But thanks for the tip John!’ Eric wandered off with that parting comment, leaving John who sighed before beginning to walk towards the guests and show them to their rooms, as was his allotted task.

Cardiff arrived the next day apologising for being late. They had come with no guiding riders and had managed to get completely lost. The pair looked flushed, dishevelled and in need of a cool bath. They introduced themselves as Jo and Zack in a very rambling way before continuing to bicker in their own tongue. John shot a look at his father, but thankfully other duties had turned his attention away from the squabbling Royals.

Now that all twelve chosen representatives were in attendance, Warwick Castle was a vibrant place, filled with all the supporters such a group would require. Only one person seemed to be thankful to return to quiet study and that was John.

# Chapter 2

# The Parade is Approaching

All the Royal parties had time to rest, unwind and get to know the surrounding areas in the days that followed. With their job of directing the Royal parties to Warwick successfully completed, the guide riders had bid them goodbye. Each one travelling back to their home county with news from the central wild. Eric and John had hoped the coming days would give them time to get to know their fellow Royals, but it had ended up with each group keeping themselves to themselves.

None had wanted to spend time with them yet there had been no feeling of hostility.

'What do they expect us to do? Look them up on the LifeMedia System (LMS) to get to know them? Have they not gained any social graces at all?' grumbled Eric.

John chuckled and shrugged. 'If they have time to place posts on LifeMedia Systems then they should head towards the nearest metallic hold! Only you would bring up social media. What's the point of knowing what someone half way round the kingdom is doing right now when you cannot help or share in the moment?' The brothers had begun walking towards the nearest market while talking. The twins knew that they were able to use the mobile systems if they wanted to, but in a way, that went against the ideals that they had been brought up with.

'Talking of which...' Commented John as his eyes scanned the distant horizon. '… you've not been away to the near hold for a while. Are you losing your curiosity for the technological?' Eric tripped slightly but didn't slow his pace.

'What? No, I don't miss all the bombardment to the senses of advertisement, holographic imagery and all that so I've not been on holiday to Coventry for a while. Last time I went it seemed the air was so oppressive...' Letting the sentence fade out, Eric glanced at his brother, to catch his eye. Eric wanted to see acceptance of his story there, but all he got was the usual calm look from John. John had not really believed his brother, but it was true that Eric had not holidayed in the metallic region for quite some time so maybe he was coming to love the natural wild, as everyone around him did.

'John, do you think they will start the training soon? The procession is weeks away and we have not even met a Walker yet! I want to get started. This waiting around is getting to me.'

'Who knows? You could always ask father. You know as well as I do that asking won't go down well and he will lecture you again on patience. But you could ask him.'

'Hmm, you're right, but I know you are as eager as I!' Eric said this with a slight smirk as he did know his brother well and could see by the slight fidgeting at quiet times that he was just as excited. As the conversation continued about what they might have to undertake as training, the market place continued with daily life around them. The people were pleasant, dressed in a variety of styles of loose fitting and flowing garments. The colour theme seemed to mainly consist of greens, browns, creams and on rare occasions, blue. Though any colour material could be purchased, the natural colours were more readily available in the wilds and seemed to fit suitably with their natural environment.

The twins' clothes were slightly more fitted but matched the local colour themes of the surrounding areas; they did not stand out. A few faces turned, but apart from a nod or a rare raised hat their presence was accepted without any pomp.

'Do you people never announce your arrival?' a voice cut into their conversation making John and Eric stop. They were surprised by the sudden presence of another Royal group, but they were not surprised by their tone. 'You wander around here, and nobody bats an eyelid! I think the only reason they look at us is because our choice in colours is far more vibrant' It was true that Simon & Liam were in quite garish purple and green, but it wasn't that much out of place.

'I think you're making a massive thing out of this Simon. Here we all work together so why should they stand to attention as we pass? Besides, that would get on my nerves after a while…' John's tone was bordering on reprimanding, but not enough to cause offence. Eric on the other hand held nothing back as he snapped at the Glaswegian Royals.

'You come here all high and mighty with your flash parade and now you are complaining about our people?'

'No, Simon didn't mean it like that it was purely an observation.' Liam had spoken quickly when he saw the expression on Eric's face.

'You keep out of this Liam. It is my point of view and I am making it; there is nothing wrong with that.' Simon raised a hand and brushed long fingers through his hair, the action almost agitated. 'I was merely saying that being Royals, the people in the area should show respect and at least acknowledge our presence with more than a nod. We are going to be their council. They are going to come to us for help and advice. We are going to be upholding their law…' Simon took a breath to continue, but John felt that Simon was getting a little above his station and his voice was starting to rise. Before any more could be said a simple raise of John's hand seemed to stop all talking. John, quietly spoke into the silence.

'...but we are not Walkers yet and here in Warwick we ask our patrons to be polite, friendly and respect each other. It is as simple as that.' It was a fact and to argue this would have caused more unrest. Simon and Liam had heard of Eric's temper the same as everyone else had and they did not feel like seeing that side of him here in the street. Straightening their shoulders, they nodded and as if passing strangers walked away at a sauntering pace.

Eric frowned at how John had silenced the brewing argument but soon shook the feeling off and chuckled at his brother.

'Points to you John. To think we are going to have to work with those guys for the next 50 years or so, it's going to be interesting!' John didn't comment because at that moment he had spotted the grey outfits of the southern party and was intrigued by what the four were doing. They had chosen to sit at a table of a local inn and were holding cards in their hands. John indicated to Eric, with a nod, that they should go over. Changing direction, the twins headed over towards the inn.

'Hi,' All four of the south west Royals greeted the twins, but didn't really catch what they had said only the gist that it was friendly.

'You both had proper trouble with Liam and Simon eh? We're keeping our heads down and keeping away from them.' Darryn shrugged and quickly turned back to the hand of cards he was holding. John should have been more interested in the game, but he was more amazed that Darryn's hair did not move in the breeze.

The twins decided that they didn't really have time to find out more about the game being played. Parting with a polite nod and comments of seeing them later they turned away and back to the market. John and Eric slowly became aware that the grass around their feet was swaying slightly; a breeze slowly increasing in intensity making the blades dance. Eric looked up to the sky and frowned, a sideways glance to John mumbling. 'A storm?' People's actions around them showed they could feel the change in temperature. Signs were being brought in or covers being placed on stock, while peoples' paces increased their eyes scanning for shelter. The boys turned to look back at the castle then hastily began to make their way home, eyes fixated on a growing cloud bank that began to shroud the turrets tips.

Once back at the castle they were confronted by the entrance hall teaming with workers, guards, farmers with deliveries and more surprisingly their father. The two ran over to him. They went to raise awareness of the brewing storm but noting his concerned expression and asked what was going on instead. Before they had chance to ask, their father silenced them with a single hand motion and answered their unspoken questions.

‘The councillors Makkan and Siska are disagreeing about who should be your tutor. The land can cope with different elements arguing. The other DragonWalkers can continue to keep the balance while the argument is resolved, but, both Makkan and Siska are masters of air. Their negative flows towards each other is causing this shift in the weather.’ He paused to look about the entrance hall and to bark a few orders to staff then continued. ‘It was so sudden that nobody really noticed it, but now, now you can almost feel the lightning that could crash at any time.’

‘Shouldn’t someone stop them?’ This was not what his father wanted to hear from Eric, and he rounded on his quick-witted son.

‘Do you think people are not trying? How do you stop two DragonWalkers when their flow is shifting towards the negatives of their power? If the other elements get involved it could cause chaos, and even then, you would still need the other pair to keep the balance. This is a lesson you should both learn here and now!!’ His hand actions accenting his final words. Frowning further and looking between John and Eric he added ‘For each element, there are two DragonWalkers. They share the duties of keeping balance of their dedicated element: earth, air, fire, water, nature and ether. Both working in harmony creates the perfect balance, one out of balance can be sustained, but both? The effect the raging elements would have if both fell from their duties I cannot imagine and do not wish to ever see it. Remember that!' On their father's final words, the storm outside had whipped up into a frenzy and the lightning that struck nearby gave only a glimpse of what could happen if this situation continued getting out of control.

John and Eric were both wide-eyed as the grey clothed Royals began to stagger their way into the entrance hall away from the market. A few words from the storm swept Royals reached John's ear. 'Destroyed that inn we were sitting in' and 'It's a bad'un!!!'. John had begun to walk towards the group to find out more, but he stopped and whirled to face the centre of the room. Everyone in the room had done similar to John because suddenly, from out of nowhere a light had begun to shimmer. Just in time, their father called 'Get back!', placing an arm across the front of the twins in a protective stance. The air in front of them seemed to fold around the light and a portal to the council room was opening. Its edges seeming like a rip in fabric, and though the council room was clear, the portal seemed to shimmer as if in a heat haze. It wasn't long before the poral stabilised and two gentlemen passed through and stood before them. The fabric of the poral closed and was gone. With that all eyes turned to the two individuals that now seemed to fill the room with their presence.

'Enough Makkan! This will do no good for anyone. We will decide a tutor by vote and that will be the end of it. Do you feel what is happening outside? How far will this argument go? Will you see the wilds flattened? Will you see the heights of Coventry fall by your hand? Calm down and get a hold of yourself.' The gentleman who spoke seemed to be in his late 60's and though his hair greyed, his shoulders hunched slightly and his legs seeming to bow under his weight, the command in his voice was intoxicating. He straightened his shoulders as much as he could and looked about the room. From his creased face eyes bored into the souls of everyone in the entrance hall. His right eye a piercing blue, his left eye had everyone looking back. His left eye held the markings of his DragonSoul and were striking against his face. Its cat like iris glaring with the colour of his DragonSoul; purple. Quietly leaning towards Liam Simon made a comment

'That's Lindany. The Purple DragonWalker. His magic is ether, I mean portals. He must have parted the two Air Walkers.' The whispering earned them a glare from Lindany but nothing more. The DragonWalker continued.

'I can feel your anger is ebbing and just in time. Not only is the inn going to have to be cleared and sorted in time for the festival, the Natural Walkers are going to have a time getting the wilds to look as nice as they did but 15 minutes ago.' Makkan looked through the front door with eyes of grey and took a deep breath. Finally, his shoulders sagged.

'I understand, but for 50 years I have put up with that air bag and my patience is not what it was. I'm tired Lindany. We all are, and I don't think this festival can come soon enough. Let some new strong minds deal with the balance.' He seemed to sag even further then and lean into the Purple Walker.

'You know. We have been lucky to live the life we have, with the magic still but a shimmer in our senses. Maybe it is growing stronger? Maybe that is what is causing my moods to crackle slightly?' The chuckle that followed was good natured as the two DragonWalkers began to head out of the entrance hall, as though nobody else was watching.

'…that is a bad excuse for your temper Makkan, and you know it. Back when you were a Royal human you were still a pain in the arse…' What was said in answer to that was lost as activity began to start up again in the main halls.

*The air around the stone had begun to pulse. The wardens of the chamber had been doubled as the stones aura had begun to grow. The metal given by the holds and the stone from the wilds seemed to be rippling; all knew it was an illusion caused by all the energy surrounding the stone and its pedestal. People on duty stood in awe as their eyes caught the colours of blue, green, red and purple mixing and moving underneath the vale that had now been placed to protect the stone from full view.*

Not far from Warwick rose the Metallic Hold of Coventry. All in its boarders were proud of how the great metropolis had turned out; bearing in mind its history of having to be rebuilt time and time again. Coventry had never once lost its heart and even to this day it was the greatest producer of the electric cars and motorbikes. Its roads and pavements cut grooves crisscrossing between its towering skyscrapers. Each one strong and bold on the skyline. Around the tower bases, teemed life as people moved like ants through the city areas, going about their business or returning home from productive days. Most people did not stop to talk or nod to a stranger. Everyone had their eyes focused on where they were going, or in most cases at the information that was being projected onto their retina data displays.

Some seemed to talk to themselves, others seemed to be moving objects about in the air that nobody else could see, possibly sending that last datafile that they failed to upload from where they worked. These seemingly involuntary actions were something that everyone accepted, it was normal to the individuals who lived in the high-tech world. Sometimes people would stop and look at a piece of advertisement that had started up on a tower wall displays, or sometimes people would stop to purchase items that would be delivered by the time they got home, but above all nobody was really looking at their surroundings.

Milli had been brought up in this metallic hold of Coventry. Her gene test had put her there to carry on with her family. Her schooling had prepared her for the life of a neuro nurse and she was looking forward to going to university to complete the cycle of her education. Even at 11 years of age she had passed the exams that showed she had the aptitude for nursing. She was strangely pleased that she was in the one job that broke the metallic boundary. She would have contact with other people on a regular basis. She was pleased that she was able to specialise in neuroscience, which had become a very specialist career path within the holds. In Milli's mind her chosen profession felt like the closest thing to growth and nature that she was going to get. She had the personality to fit the role. She was hard working and thankfully she had the aptitude to study. Milli had no striking features. She was not skinny or overweight, not particularly tall or short. Her mousy brown hair always fell about her face in a messy bob, which suited her slightly pale complexion.

Right now, Milli had lost herself in the VR (Virtual Reality) world of Morla. It was a fully immersive world based on her favourite Japanese Anime. Though you never saw the original characters from the show as you interacted with new characters that people had created, in your mind you could imagine that the famous characters were off causing havoc somewhere while you wandered through the streets, stopped at the shops or spent time following the canal routes. You could follow adventures or fill your time watching the scenery slowly change. Milli had a friends list but all were AFK (away from keyboard – though you didn't need a keyboard anymore, the term from the original MMORPG games, was still used). Her avatar was sitting in a café watching a noob (a new gamer) try not to fall into the water of the canal and they looked like they were only just getting used to walking. She didn't realise she was that close to the starting area, so whoever this guy was must have really struggled to get this far towards the town.

While glancing at the clear blue sky and the distant rolling hillside Milli had made the decision to go and help the young man learn how to walk, virtually, when a notification appeared on the right-hand side of her vision. It scrolled into her consciousness and burst the illusion of her virtual haven. Sighing she read the notice from her father stating that her dinner was ready. Milli looked down at the mint tea she had on the table before her, took a last sip then went to her log out menu and clicked to leave.

On returning to reality, Milli's vision was filled with the sharp edges of metal and the shimmering of glass. She was lucky, her parents were well respected in their professions, so they lived high up on the 73rd floor of a central tower. It possibly made no difference to a lot of people but to Milli it meant she had a view with less advertising. The lower levels could have advertisements scrolling on all windows, at all times of day and night. Placing her VR headset on her bedside table she stretched and began to rise from her bed. In comparison to the rest of her house, and possibly the whole tower, her room was filled with soft pastel furnishings which helped calm her mind. She took time to glance at the view outside before getting herself ready and heading out to the dining area. Both her parents looked up from where they sat, at the table, and smiled. Their expressions looking slightly wrong compared to the crisp grey of their business style clothing. Her mother spoke first

'We thought we had lost you again today. No status updates, no pictures of where you were. Tell us, what have you been up to?'

Milli sat down at her place and began to answer her mother's question.

'It was my day off today, so I didn't really do anything of note.' By the time she had finished her sentence both parents were looking down at their meals, and more importantly, to the vast embedded screen that made up the table. Knowing the conversation was over, Milli too, looked at her own section of the screen. Her fork worked automatically as she began to look through the updates of the people she had on her friends and family contacts list. Her father's company had celebrated a milestone of the most electric cars in circulation, a feat she could not imagine the numbers of. Her mother had had a busy day of sales of her designer sleek fitting suits.

Milli had to admit that the meal, she was absently eating, was good. It wasn't the normal take away orders that were selected from the vast collection of online restaurants, no, this was good. Though she enjoyed the flavour of her mint tea, VR food never quite satisfied. Her mind drifted back to her VR haven but with a different twist of thought. Real life was one thing and Virtual Reality was something different entirely. You could have your own avatar and life in there, but how people could choose to live their life full time in the virtual world she could never understand. To be placed on a bed, wired into bodily function supporting machines to then live your life in your mind? She could understand the elderly, the bed bound, the infirm but not all the others who were her age or older. She had no answer for her own thoughts so turned back to the meal and savoured the roasted beef for the delicacy that it was. This brought her up short, because beef was a delicacy!

Finishing her mouthful, she looked from one parent to another.

'What's the special occasions? Is it your car sales?' her father cleared his mouth and smiled.

'Ahh you read that? Yes, that was a special occasion, but I've done some updates since then. You really do need to keep up with your feeds.' Wiping his mouth with a tissue he continued. 'no, no. Tonight, you are the special occasion. Yes, let me finish' he added as he saw the protest rising. 'You might not have published how well you have done at college, but the institution has and with your score ranking we know you will do well.' Sip of wine taken he then continued. 'So, the LifeMedia Systems grape vine has told us of a rare occasion that is taking place. It only happens every 50 years, and this one happens to co-inside with your $18^{th}$ birthday.' Milli's mum nodded and both seemed to wait for the penny to drop. As there was no sign of this happening they sighed. 'You never do watch the news feeds, do you?' her father continued with his bass tones showing the excitement that was beginning to get infectious. There was a drawn-out pause.

'Go on…' prompted Milli, then thinking about the updates her dad mentioned she quickly turned to her screen. She sifted through her media feeds with the skill and speed of anyone brought up with technology. Her fingers stopped. '…a vacation?'

'Yes. In the wilds of Warwick, the DragonSoul procession will be happening. Though both your mother and I feel it is an unhealthy interest you have with those places. For your $18^{th}$ and with such grades we are willing to put that aside and we will go on vacation for the parade.' Before Milli could ask any questions, her mother added.

'...but I will need to be back by 8pm. This day out will mess with my production schedule and I have some ladies from Bristol who are travelling here for a private viewing the next day.' A full days' vacation? And into the wilds? For the first time in a long time Milli did not know what to say so she did the one thing she knew would make her parents happy.

She updated her status: 'Into the wilds.'

# Chapter 3

# Behind the Balance

The frayed tempers of the Air Walkers had put people on edge. The workers, trying to get everything in place for the ceremony; the leading family, knowing they must get their affairs in order; the guardians, needing to make sure their charges are in good health and lastly, the inn keeper had to get his walls fixed and his inn habitable for visitors. In his lifetime, this was the only occasion a group of metallic hold people had booked rooms!! Ray, the inn keeper, was not the only person to be experiencing visiting metallic holders; the castle had some of Coventry and Birmingham's governing bodies staying for the ceremony. Several families, who's ties to the metallic world, by blood or business also had people arriving for the ceremony. It was an unheard-of mix, accepted due to the occasion being so rare.

It had been a few days since the storm and Ray was standing outside observing the wreckage that a bolt of lightning and high winds had caused to his beloved inn. The inn's roof had been predominantly thatch, with slate and tile work where the thatch had worn away, but now it had blackened edges and crumpled slate. The thatching was a major issue as it was a lost skill. Ray feared that the beaming that were left raw would not hold any other material in place and what could replace his beloved thatch anyway? His inn looked sad and ruined. Days had past and all the workers Ray had contacted, to help with the repairs, had been busy. The metallic families would be heading this way in a matter of weeks and he at least, wanted them to see the more comfortable side of the wilds. Slouching his shoulders and shaking his head, he slowly went indoors. The inn was homely, in a dark and 'oldish' way.

The walls stone, the floor slate and the bar area a beautiful piece of oak. The chairs and seating area were in no order or style, and his customers tended to always sit in the chair that suited them the best. The curling on a sofa type, the sitting at a table with elbows propping their drink type, the leaning back lazy type, they all found a place that suited them and that's what he liked. He knew most of the drinks his regulars ordered, and this helped him stay in business; only buying in the brews that were most popular, with a few rarer delicacies kept behind the bar for special occasions. The bar downstairs, the kitchens out the back and the front seating area were the main places still standing, which he thanked the magic for, otherwise, he would have no business at all! The upper floors were either scorched, damaged or swept into chaos.

'No luck Ray?!' Said one of his regulars.

'Nah, I've asked about but unless I go further afield everyone is booked up with work for the festivities.' He poured himself a half of ale and inhaled the fumes. 'I'll think of something… we got time…' Once Ray finished speaking, he downed the half. His actions showing that his inner stress didn't match his words, but his regulars were not going to argue with what he said. Placing the glass down on the bar, he slowly began to clean.

Ray had only just begun his cleaning/calming routine when two gentlemen walked in. Registering that they were not his regular clients Ray felt that their very presence seemed to demand attention, though they appeared relaxed.

'Can I hel…' Ray began to say but as they entered the light fully and it quickly became clear why Ray could not finish the sentence.

'No sir, we can help you.' The two approached the bar and held out their hand in the respectful greeting of equals. 'My name is Zyman and I am the Nature DragonWalker. This is Tellany, who is Earth.' They indicated each other with a hand gesture. They let Ray gain composure then nodded to continue. 'Your inn was the only building struck by lightning, all others took a beating from the stormy weather, but they have stayed strong and secure. There is no way your inn would have stood a chance. Several of the visiting Royals where here in your bar when the storm hit.

They have spoken of how you helped others around you just to turn and see your own place burn.' Zyman paused for a moment to look around the inn, nodding to several regulars who had stopped drinking to listen. Looking back to Ray he continued. 'So! We have come to help. If you would give us some time and clear the area, we should be able to put your place back into order. Probably not as pretty, architecture is not our strong point, but it will be unique!' Ray was not sure who was persuading whom, but he was not about to argue and hastily cleared the bar.

The area around the inn began to crackle with excitement. The regulars who had left the inn were now a semicircle of spectators, growing in numbers as people nearby had become curious. The crowds' whisper, like a quiet buzz, accenting the nerves Ray was feeling. Nobody could feel the magic, only the DragonWalkers, but without realising people were beginning see it. The colours seemed brighter, the sun feeling a little warmer while the grass swayed against the breeze. In the centre of the semicircle, two Walkers stood with their eyes closed. Few had seen the slow transformation that occurred when a DragonWalker used their powers, but it was a known fact that as their elements were used, depending on the effort required, more of the man would become dragon. Their left eye was always the colour of the dragon whose soul they were given but now, as the onlookers watched, the pair's hands, raised towards the inn, began to take on a different form. Fingers, frail with age, now swelled and glistening with scales, nails stretched to talons, thick and yellow. Their arms now muscular right up and under the clothes that covered their shoulders. Zyman was shimmering with scales of green while Tellany, brown. Each one had their eyes open and focused on what they were doing. Even though this transformation was something to behold, the people watching slowly turned their eyes to the inn. Stone, soil and dirt all seemed to be melding together; rippling from the surrounding area to merge with walls, filling in gaps and stabilising its base. A tree had risen from the ground behind the inn, its roots and branches seeming to merge with the back wall, travel around the outsides and cling to its every surface. As it climbed the heights of the inn's roof it looked like the tree was pulling the inn into its vast embrace. Once the branches above the roof had fanned out, the top of the tree arced forward and lowered its limbs onto the roof, beginning to lace its branches together, unnaturally, across the surface. As people watched, the tree cycled through all four seasons repeatedly, building a layer of foliage as thick as the thatch before it. The noise of nature being manipulated slowly calmed as movement came to a stop and everything settled.

The two Walkers stopped what they were doing and admired their work. Suddenly Zyman chuckled and with a sweep of his hand a final branch extended, lowering itself to beside the door. With a wink at the inn keeper he picked up the inn's sign and hung it from the very branch he had placed there. The moment was over, Ray faced two older gentlemen once more. He held out his hands and shook their now human ones with such gratitude.

‘I cannot thank you enough. Is there anything I can do in return?’ The two Walkers looked at each other, shrugged and smiled.

‘We could certainly go an ale if you have some?’

Ray took a moment to blink away his surprise

‘Of course!’ and led them into the inn, life went back to normal as people continued their daily lives.

With the balance of the elements seeming back in order, and the damage being repaired throughout Warwick, the Air Walkers who had started all the problems, had decided on who was going to tutor the group. Makkan had won the argument. The Royals had been gathered in a large teaching area, to the side of the library. Nobody was sure if this room had been an extension built into the castle for this very reason but, compared to the halls, they all knew, this room was light, airy, its paint works soft and devoid of any pictures. Large windows ran down one side, with the view of the rolling farmland beyond. In the distance you could make out a few trees and hills before the first shards of the metallic towers blocked anything else and Coventry took away the horizon with its metallic surface. Each of the chosen Royals were sat upon large cushions, on the floor, in a semicircle with their backs straight, their legs crossed and their hands resting on each knee; all had their eyes closed.

'As you now know, the balance we hold is of the elements around us. These elements are important for both metallic holds and our homeland wilds. All respect the elements and the balance is sacred. Our argument the other day was a timely reminder of this balance and how important it is that, above any other job, role or position you hold, this will be your duty. Meditation is the key to gaining balance within and only then can you truly understand the bigger picture, the natural balance and eventually the elements you will use. Though you feel you have read this story many times, learn patience as I tell you the full history of the DragonSoul.' Makkan noted a couple of the Royals twitched and signed. He had concerns over Eric, Simon and Liam which he hoped would be eased as all continued their training. He composed himself in a similar pose to the students and began to speak in a calm voice, barely a whisper, but you could hear every word.

'Dragons never perished. They were around when myths and legends were borne, they circled the skies while gods fought, but, as science and technology began to rule man's minds, they slumbered and slipped into the very legends they had played with. Magic had not been felt by man for a long time as the dragons still had the strength to keep the balance. Those who pretended to use it were just that pretending. The dragons spoke of witches, warlocks, mages and wizards holding no power. The dragons kept their own council, and while they began to slowly age and decay they learnt many wisdoms and realised that the balance of the elements and nature was the fundamental life force and that couldn't be lost. Time past, 1700s, 1800s, 1900s and with each year mankind continued to drag its feet through the world. They helped themselves to feel better with breakthroughs in technology, awards for famous people giving everyone something to strive towards, making money for comfort, flight, space flight, cars, trains, houses, chemicals, weapons, all helping man to feel in control, to feel better but man would never feel whole. But magic would not lie dormant for ever and the dragons knew that the energy was building up around them, and they were in no fit state to continue to be the wielders for ever. Their concerns grew. What would happen if one of them were to die and the magic go to the corrupted? Someone with the power of the weapons, or someone with the wealth to overthrow others. Would they give that up to work with the magic of the world? Would they understand the power they had been given? Would they become a superhero or a supervillain? The magic the dragons held, if misused, could destroy the fabric of the world and beyond. Finally, the dragons realised that they could not let this continue and were afraid of what would happen if they allowed themselves to die and the balance of the world's elements lost. As the result of their concerns, the dragons devised a plan, a promise to the world that they would not allow this to happen and they would support humanity. The time was never right. Nobody believed in dragons any more, they had left it too long. Each time they tried to make contact, the story and hype lead to that person being bombarded by the media and nobody was every believed. Then, in the 20th Century, things began to turn in a way nobody expected. Faith had splintered into many different factions. Man was fighting man but, many others were calling for peace. People began looking for space to breath, places where there was no technological noise. By 2017 the divide had triggered the path that would lead us to where we are today. During this time the dragons made their final move and approached six families from across the country. Though we did not know it at the time, the places they were drawn to, had more people with the heart and soul of the wilds and so they solidified the rights of the Royal families you are now sitting with and the cities that succumbed to nature seemed to have the growth of nature accelerated.' Though everyone had remained silent this statement caused a stir as nobody had realised this. 'I understand what you are thinking. If the dragons had not chosen those places, would the metallic world include one extra City? We cannot know how the paths would have been changed, but for you, you would not be sitting here, nor your homes be the natural birthplaces of all the Walkers in the council.' Makkan stretched his back slightly and shifted his right foot to get comfortable once more before he continued. 'Each dragon approached their chosen person and said the same matter of fact words…

*'I stand before you as one of the last remaining of my kind. I keep the balance of the elements with my brothers, yet our bodies are dying from age and decay. I would like to make a deal with you. As my body passes away to nourish the earth, my soul will stay contained in a stone along with my brothers. When two of your children turn 18 years of age, they will stand before the stone and a soul will be gifted and with it the power to control an element. With the power he holds he can help keep your lands safe, he will bring wealth and support for your people, but he will have the power and the wisdom of a dragon. This power will be his for 50 years. At which point a new generation of guardians will hold the balance of the elements. This next generation I will leave the choice to*

*man, but the lineage must be of this family. Do you accept this offer?'*

...each father thought about their young sons and discussed the matter with them. They only had days to decide and all bar one family accepted the mantle. The family to decline was Dorset, and to this day the area stands in limbo, a wild which is often forgotten.' Makkan paused a moment to get his breath before he finished the story.

'On the year of the chosen son's 18th birthday all came to the stones resting place in Warwick Castle. There they embraced the life that you hear of today by standing in front of the stone and accepting the soul with an open mind and an open heart. They became the Council of the Walkers and protect the balance through their meditation, their calm minds and the wisdom they were given. The dragon is still there, whispering, communing and supporting the man, but nobody has ever known the soul to come to the fore'. He stopped talking then and opened his eyes. Looking around the room, he noted that all eyes were on him and none of the group had been meditating on his voice at all. He shook his head and then chuckled. ‘Ok, ok, questions?’ All put their hands up and he answered them one by one. ‘No, you cannot choose the soul, it chooses you.’ ‘No, you cannot choose which element is yours either.’ ‘The natural dragons are the most powerful and the leaders of the groups. By controlling nature, they have a little bit of all the elements within them. Their role is to lead and to support any element that might be failing. They feel the power of all four: earth, air, fire and water so they have the power to boost one as required, or calm another.’ The questions kept on coming. ‘Ahh yes, the purple ones. We were surprised by these dragons from the start but the message that we received was, in the changing world you needed transport.’ Eric piped up then, and in a very offensive tone added ‘so they have no real power then?’ Makkan was on this like a shot. ‘Did you not see yesterday? They are the tempers. They are the guardians, the protectors. They can help you survive a battle or disappear into thin air. They can call you to help or split an argument…’ he ended the last comment with a wry smile.

'Their magic is unique but as we are not able to be in several places at once with the portals they provide, they are invaluable!' There were a few more questions about the colours before John raised his hand.

'Why two? It is almost like there are two teams. Two nature, two air and so on. Why?' Makkan looked at John and the pupil in his dragonic eye seemed to become as thin as ice.

'That is a very good question John. This was something that was never really explained to us by the original dragons, but we feel that the reason is simple. The human body is not as robust as the dragon within. Our bodies can be injured, hurt, broken. The balance must not be, so, although the natural soul can heal the human flesh and patch you back together again, while this is happening, the balance must be continued. Normally the duties are shared, one person in the central council hall meditating, calming and channelling the balance while the other is away, resting, helping their people with problems, visiting the metallic holds… and then the rolls are reversed. At times of council meetings, we are all as one and can feel the shift and support each other, or, at times of great torment, all can work together. If I am honest with you, you do not need to be in the council chamber to hold the balance. Keep calm and the peace will work for you and the magic will flow. But it is not worth the risk. Get two of you in a situation where you become agitated and well, again, the other day was the perfect example of what can happen.' Makkan snorted then and smiled 'In short answer, yes, two teams'.

Makkan really had the group's attention now and each question was getting more serious as the group realised the roles they had taken on and what it truly meant. It was a daunting task and the mood was growing tense. Tanya raised her hand.

'Sir. My family have sent me as I am the only other Royal bar Johan, in Truro, who is of age. Why have they only been males before?' This question took a little thought and Makkan sat quietly to think. Absently his cushion raised off the ground on a swirl of wind. It just showed how natural it had become for him to be one with his element.

‘As far as we know, all dragons approached the fathers of the children they were giving their souls to. If we go back through the ages, roles were not as diverse as they are now and perhaps the fathers took it that it had to be sons? For whatever reason we are not sure why this happened, but we are glad to see a change for the better.’

Eventually Makkan raised his hands to stem the tide of questions.

‘There is still time for more questions another day as the procession is not yet upon us. In the time to come, you will study how to accept the soul, how to commune with the soul and hear its wisdom, more history and finally some defence practice. You need to be prepared for any eventuality. But for now, there has been a lot to take in. Clear your minds, rest, eat, and I will begin more training tomorrow.’

# Chapter 4

# Get Your Head in the Game

Come on Milli! Get your head in the game. Don't slip out of Virtual Reality on me now!' Shouted the game leader. At these words Milli snapped to attention and panicked. Half her raid group were dead, and the other half needed some serious healing. Her co-healer, who was also the group leader, was sweating, panting and drastically running out of mana. To get her back in the game he added,

‘I can’t heal a ten-man raid on my own you know! I’ll be blaming you not the rogue or hunter if we wipe!!’ Those last joking threats got her fired up and she got back to healing where she could. It took some doing, with swords clashing, people shouting, spells flying and the odd grunting sounds from the boss, but they managed to complete the area and enjoyed picking from the loot dropped. As the group was resurrected by the two healers, they began stand together, the dead boss discarded to the side. The plate wearing tank who had died rolled his shoulders as he walked towards the group.

‘I still can’t get over the creepy feeling when your waiting for ‘rez’!! No leaving the screen to go make a drink, waiting for that Healer to resurrect you, like the old keyboard days… so, Milli, I would rather not die. It’s also ruining my hard-earned reputation as a staying alive kind of tank’. Straightening his shoulders and sheathing his mace and shield, he was building himself up to continue when he was cut off by her fellow healer. Waving his staff to distract him he said

'Come on tank, don't blame her. She has had her head in the clouds since finding out she is heading into the wilds for the parade…' A few in the group nodded in agreement. The tank bowed and shook his head for a moment before grinning, raising a fist in the air and laughing. 'Ten-man raid completed with only one healer...oh yeah!'

The statement from the tank got the group all talking at once in the fun after fight banter. As statistics and damage-per-second levels were talked about amicably the almost wipe became a fun topic to jest about later. The group was a sight that nobody could imagine: Elves, dwarves, wolves, humans and strange beasts standing in a room that looked like an Egyptian landscape. Each one dressed in a collage of plate, cloth, leather and mail. The games in the metallic holds had moved on to the next level of Virtual Reality whereby the players are able to take part in the full immersive experience. Someone piped up with

'So who wants to try the next level? I hear there is a legendary staff and shield that drops up there…'. All were up for it but Milli raised her hand.

‘I’m sorry guys, I’d love to but looking at the time, I have ten minutes to get to class!!’.

‘Oh, come on, that’s plenty of time to do this floor. We all know the mechanics, right? We have been working on this as a guild!’ Milli shook her head and chuckled.

‘You know I can’t switch as easily as you can!’ Time is everything in the modern city and if you can switch from one task straight to another without an issue, you can save precious time and be seen as far more productive but Milli was unable to do this, she just needed a few moments to clear her mind and get ready for the next task.

On that thought Milli logged out of her game but not from the Virtual Reality platform. She stood for a moment in front of her vast desktop of glass panels floating around her. All the programmes she used on a regular basis spanning around her in an accessible semicircle, images of their main function or logo shimmering on the crystal-like surface. Remembering her resolve to her family, she walked toward her social media portal and updated her status: ‘Almost an epic raid fail. Saved by the bell, but now onto college.’. Taking a deep breath and closing her eyes Milli took a moment to clear her mind from the buzz of the game, to allow herself to balance her thoughts before she finally opened her eyes, turned to the shimmering glass panel of her university pane and clicked load.

A few moments later, Milli's avatar walked into a sterile environment with all the sounds and smells associated with a Hospital. Her clothes had changed to that of a student wearing jeans, an olive green top covered with an open uniform white coat. She smiled and greeted the five others who had entered the room. The last two leaned over to whisper to Milli that she should have stayed for the last floor, it had been brilliant. Milli shook her head smiling.

'I don't know how you do it….' She would have gone on to ask if they had managed to do their updates at the same time, but the professor had arrived, and the class was beginning. In front of them was an avatar of a body lying on a stainless-steel table. A glass dome, hung over the person, giving them dignity where required but enabling the group to see from head to toe. Seemingly imbedded in the glass were figures of vital signs, images of internal nervous systems and organs mapped out in fine detail. The heart beating deep red and the lungs inflating steadily in a light blue. Each of the students clapped their hands together once, then as they slowly pulled their hands apart, a keyboard formed between them. Once the clapping motion was completed the keyboard hung in the space where it had formed and allowed each student to input the stats and outcomes for the session, along with any notes and coding within the classroom space.

'Milli!!' The professor pulled her up by making her jump. 'We are focusing on the C6/C7 area, not the T6! For goodness sake, I want you to look at the nuclius-pulposis within the intervertebral discs of that area. Is it damaged?' There was enough of a frown in her tutor's tone to get Milli back on track, her fingers zipping across the glass keyboard and the coding beginning to scroll in with the others of the class. 'Good, now that all of you are focused…' and so the class continued.

Finally, when it was over, Milli ripped the VR headset off and slowly began to turn her head left to right. Running her hands through her hair, she cleared the strap marks left by the headset. Her hands then wandered down to slowly begin to remove the sensory straps around upper arm and upper legs which help capture the limb signals making the virtual world totally immersive. Once the sensor straps had been removed, she stretched out and relaxed. To think that some people have gone to the extreme of having the sensors inserted permanently! Replying to her parents that she was in her room but needed to quickly purchase some clothes for packing, Milli then did something unheard-of in this technological world. Standing she walked over to a home-made calendar and, with a pen meant for whiteboards, she crossed off another day and smiled. Only two days left.

Warwick seemed as though it was reaching its capacity. The market area now had stalls open every day with the demand on stocks ever present. Deliveries of food, drinks and general living staples being requested daily from suppliers. The houses and inns that were welcoming visitors filling fast and the junction into the wilds from the great superslab motorways, which were the veins between the metallic holds, was now seeing the first reduction in traffic speed for an age. A collaboration between the nearby metallic holds and the Warwick wilds had reached a peak never heard of before when the main junction to Warwick and the road that flowed from it had all been reconnected to the motor system with new tarmac. The council conceded that it was necessary if they were to make the parade day inclusive. The new road now snaked its way for a short while, stopping where a multi-story carpark had been erected. The electric points for the vehicles attached, the systems for security added and a stables block beside it to allow the guide riders to support people's transition from tarmac to track and a completely different speed of life. The main route that the DragonSoul Stone was going to take from vault to council hall had been marked out with flags, bunting and, as used on other very rare occasions, an old orange cone that had been kept for such events. People were everywhere either going about their normal daily life but with an air of excitement, or with a slightly lost expression as they look for places to eat, drink and take in all the wonders that the wilds of Warwickshire can offer. Throughout all, Ray's newly built inn was doing a roaring trade!

About the same time as Milli was focusing on her shopping, the second stage of the lessons were being undertaken by the young Royals. They had spent much time in study, learning the history of the wilds, the hereditary of the systems of their world, to understand more of the metallic holds and skills needed to lead. They had also spent much time spent learning non-violent-crisis intervention, how to council and activities to help balance the mind. Most had found this dull, but all had enjoyed the defence classes. The group of twelve had worked hard to master hand to hand combat, sword skills, archery and a defensive art which is a combination of Karate and Kick boxing. Today though, they were back in the airy classroom, each sat on a bean bag with their legs crossed and each Royal focusing on the lesson before them. There seemed to be a low pressure forming as Air Walker Makkan was helping to slow their breathing for a calming state of mind.

'Now, you have all been excelling in your studies and I commend you on your physique, but today, we must begin your journey of heart and soul. The final journey before the fast-approaching merging of souls. You need to be ready to accept the gift you have been given but also, to be ready to give yourself to the DragonSoul as you become one. You must be at peace with the understanding that you are sharing your life with the dragon. When the time comes for you to accept the dragon soul you must do so with an open mind and heart. You need to be willing to share your strengths and weaknesses. Yes Simon, weaknesses! You must be willing to learn and to grow. You need to be willing to work with and learn from the soul. In doing so, you become more powerful than you can imagine...and, I think I'm quoting from a film when I say, 'with power comes responsibility'. He was about to go on when a movement caught his attention. 'Yes Eric?'. Eric had raised his hand and stood to ask his questions.

'What happens if you do not accept the soul?'. A slight worry flickered across the Walker's eyes but he hid it well. 'As far as we are aware, you would be at war in your own body. You would have access to the power but not the skill to control it to its full potential, meaning that you would not be stable when supporting your element...'

'And that's just a theory?'

'yes'

'All this has never been proven?'

'No'

'So it comes down to you controlling the soul and it liking You?'

'Yes...'

'And once the dragon soul is in you the deal is sealed?'

'Yes'

'And this information was given...'

'Enough Eric!' flared the Air Walker, his iris reducing to the smallest of slits. 'All of this you can read in the teaching books you have available to you. This is not the time or the place...John if this is another irritating question, I swear I'll throw a hurricane under your arse....' John leaned away from the anger apparent on their masters' face but still managed to stand to ask his question.

'No sir. I just have one question. What happens to you after the ceremony? As you will lose your connection?' Silence fell over the group. All looking between Makkan and John with awe or concern, waiting for their tutor's reaction. The DragonWalker spoke, but his voice was not the sure crisp instructor, but the slight shaking of an older gentleman unsure of their future.

'We do not know John. On the day of the ceremony, the DragonSoul Stone will be placed at the centre of the council room. During the procession, no one will be allowed to touch it or look directly at it. The stone will be covered by a vail. We thought about encasing it in iron, but with so many people coming to see the procession, we felt that a veil would allow people to see the stone's shimmering light, now active, and catch the outline of it's magnificence. I digress. When the stone is placed at the centre of the council chamber, we twelve Walkers will step forth and place our hands upon it, you twelve chosen will do the same. Using the power within the stone the souls will pass from us to you. You will then enter a dreamlike state and there you will meet your dragon and the binding process will begin. For some it is swift and will be as though you are in harmony from the start; for others it will take more time. As for us, we are not sure, but we hope we have time to return to our beloved homes and rest before slipping from this world. We fear that the transition might be hard as we will be losing a part of ourselves.' He paused for a moment before smiling reassuringly at the group about him adding 'but we will soon find out.' This honesty seemed to strike a chord far more than the description given in previous reading. 'Do not worry yourself. We believe the dragon souls will merge with you and you will become the new age of Walkers. Your souls will carry on all the lessons we could give, they understand the magic and the balance and will give you all the guidance you need. The council's support keeps our records and will be available to you at any time, but it is time for new eyes, new minds and new souls to guide the balance.'

The session went on in a far more practical sense after the questions and answers. The DragonWalker spoke of his first months of bonding - how he had spent many nights communing with his dragon as they became one; how he still feels his presence and can ask for his guidance at any time and has learnt to understand the feelings and emotions that form a level of communication when awake; or the long conversations he has had verbally when in a meditative state. He spoke of the affinity with his chosen element, the feeling of absolute joy when standing with fellow Walkers and keeping the balance, or when feeling the magic flow through your body as you wield that magic to support others. All were listening keenly, and finally they felt ready to accept the gift and the burden - finally understanding that there was more to the bond than mechanics, but that it meant the forging of a friendship of love and respect.

# Chapter 5

# The Long-Awaited Day

Eyes bright with excitement watched the world pass by. Milli sat in the back of her father's car transfixed by the passing views. The metallic family had begun the day like any other: breakfast, checking the news feeds, confirming evening meetings and, where Milli was concerned, looking at the view from her window and trying to see past the sharp edges of Coventry. From the moment she had woken, her imagination had been working overtime about what the day might hold. She had made sure her phone was charged to the maximum, her extra battery pack full and ready to go. Milli had chosen clothes she hoped would fit in with the wilds colour theme and she felt ready for this holiday. She very rarely made such an effort, but today *she* was going on an adventure, not her avatar.

Milli had not realised just how vast Coventry was. The sun's rays glistened off one building then the next, accentuating their sharp corners and rippling glass surfaces. Part of her mind noticed the coming and going of people all about her, but that paled into insignificance when her eyes caught sight of the upcoming superslab. In the early 21$^{st}$ Century the massive motorways had been widened and reinforced and become the life blood between the different metallic holds. Tarmac had become a scarce commodity, but science had found a way of grinding plastic, compressing it and infusing it into the road surfaces. At first this had caused major accidents as the new surfaces were not compatible with the cars of the time, but now they helped to speed up the vehicles as the lack of resistance from the surface worked with the slide tech. It was the turning point of manufacturers going from petrol/diesel engines to the electric ones used today. The plastic gave the superslab a glistening effect and a feeling of gliding to any destination. In the front of the car her mother sat in one of her sleek suits, seeming to swipe at the air. Milli knew she was working on the designs for her evening meeting. Her dad, in his fitted black suit, also sat in the front of the automated car, with the glass iPad that accompanied him anywhere. He had been making notes at different points throughout the journey. Milli presumed that this was an effective way to check that his designs were working as he'd hoped.

As Milli's eyes drifted from sight to sight, she fell into silence to admire the outside world, keeping the running commentary on the views in her mind. As Coventry came to an end and the horizon suddenly opened out before her, she could not help but gasp - the haven of her MMORPG Morla flashing before her eyes as she soaked up the expanse of colour that hit her senses. Like theatre curtains, the striking buildings around her slowly began to draw away from the road, opening to fields coloured green and yellow with crops, swaying in the breeze. Great trees reached for the sky with nothing to stop them, and finally her eyes caught a glint of light hitting what she assumed was Birmingham. Leaning forward between the seats, Milli pointed to the shard on the horizon.

'Birmingham was famous for its rail industry, wasn't it? And for being the hub of the civil rights movement?' Her raised hand still pointing into the distance to explain her sudden question. Her father looked up from his workings and nodded.

'Well yes, the railroad parks that tie in with Birmingham New Street are famous for their flawless design, but really, Birmingham was famous, in its day, for the canal system and its waterways. It is said that it had more canals than Venice!' Her father's head nodded to confirm the fact. Milli pulled one of those faces which show it really was surprising: mouth pulled down at the corners, eyebrows raised and a slow nod of the head.

'I'll look it up, that's interesting...'. She leaned back into her seat, but her eyes were soon back on the rolling patchwork fields rather than the information on her digital retinal display.

After what felt like days, rather than hours, all were aware that the vehicle was slowing down. The glass that covered the front of the vehicle to allow you to see out now had directions overlaid on its surface showing they were about to leave the superslab. While the car made the appropriate speed alterations, Milli's dad went into details of how no expense was spared on bringing the Warwick junction up to spec to enable car travel with the consent of the council and the governors. The car began to wind its way on the smooth new road before reaching the allotted parking space. Milli felt that the car park looked so out of place and was an eyesore against the wilds around them, which was completely the opposite of her mother's reaction.

'Just look at it Tony, it so... so... unorganised!' - look of disgust on her face. Before she turned away, she lowered her voice so that only Tony could hear and asked with a strain in her voice, 'Is this really what - *she* - wants?'

Tony frowned and very slightly nodded his head. He was not entering that conversation now, but his eyes drifted to Milli and he smiled, his eyes showing the love he felt for his daughter as he watched her rapt expression, her head turning this way and that to take everything in. Once it was safe to leave the vehicle, the three holders got their first true taste of the wilds. They walked out of the car park and stood on the last bit of road and were met by a wooden trailer with several horses attached.

There had been effort made with this cart. Tony had to admit that the carpentry was superb, with the dovetailed joints holding an intricate pattern from the lovingly cut wood. The sturdy wheels had spokes perfectly spaced for balance. Steps were placed at the back of the trailer and, as they got in, Tony continued to admire the craftmanship that created comfortable seating with enough space to hold up to twelve. Helping them into the trailer was one of the guide riders. He had come from Leeds.

'Good evening sir, ma'ams. Welcome to Warwick. You're in good hands here: this trailer was commissioned especially for this day.' That got Milli's dad's attention, and the conversation turned to how they had the skills to craft in wood, did they think about the balance of the cart on the ground? … It did make Milli chuckle: her dad had always been fascinated with anything that moved, but then that's why he was the leading manufacturer of electric cars. Once they were sat down, Milli's mum taking a long time to get comfortable, the guide stood on the edge and smiled.

'As I said, you are in safe hands here. These fine horses travelled with the Royals from Leeds. I had the opportunity to go back or stay, and I wasn't about to miss the opportunity of seeing the parade. Now, if anything spooks these horses, I'm going to have to focus on them, so please accept my apologies for raising my voice and the bumpy ride that might ensue. Also, these are the wilds so please keep your hands well within this trailer. We wouldn't want a tree to catch your arm or a bramble to scrape your eye.' In the virtual world, the surroundings couldn't hurt you, so this was a new concept, and Milli was not sure if she was anxious about this or more excited. 'You have got places booked at an inn, so we are going straight there. Warwick is busy at this time, but we should get there in plenty of time so you can have some time to rest before the parade. Ray has a delightful selection of ales you might be interested in…' With a jolt, the horses took their first step and the trailer began its trundling progress. Milli caught sight of other riders placed near the trailer and assumed this was a safety precaution – but from what? Milli was amazed at all the things she had never experienced in her life just on the short journey from carpark to inn: pot holes, the rustling of leaves, the sound of other animals wandering nearby, the smell of horse sweat, the noise of wood grating on dirt. All kept her in a state of wonder.

After a short while the surroundings cleared, and Warwick Castle came into view. Even though the houses and market streets were a wonder, it was the castle in the distance that made her gasp again! Grabbing her mum by the shoulder, Milli pointed to the building of stone.

'There it is!'

'Yes dear' was not the response she wanted, but looking at her phone, she caught a glimpse of her mum's update and realised she was just as much in awe.

'Oh, we still have signal!' the comment caught the attention of the gentleman leading the trailer who called back over his shoulder. The wind caught most of what he said and blew the words away from her hearing, but she got the idea that Warwick was still on the network as were most major wild cities, but they only chose to use it to access supplies and to keep contact with the metallic holds in times of emergency.

Ray welcomed the family to the inn with a warm smile and open arms. His smile would be ever etched on Milli's memory as he explained that the rooms were ready and cleaned, that he would happily serve them a meal after the festivities and that they were welcome to sit outside and take in the sights.

While the family made themselves comfortable, on the outskirts of the city two DragonWalkers had arrived at the

DragonSoul Stone's resting place and were preparing for its transportation. The Purple DragonWalker, Lindany, had just opened a portal, from the castle, which he and Makkan had walked through. The guards on hand bowed respectfully then stood to attention, their uniforms and swords looking sharp.

'Has the transport arrived?' asked Lindany. Hearing a positive response, he turned to the Air Walker and sighed. 'I'm not comfortable with this! Why the parade - why not transport it directly to the chamber? Anything could go wrong.' He frowned, placing his hands on his hips before continuing. 'Oh, I know I was out-voted on this and all want to give people the show they want. What was it? reviving the legends of us in people's minds? But really, this is very risky.'

'Nobody knows what would happen if it were to go wrong. You're making a mountain out of this' noted Makkan; roles were reversed from last time the pair had been seen.

'I might be at that, but at least it would be safe, simple and quiet.'

'You worry too much. The people will be too scared of what would happen if they touched it, and the veil is thick enough to stop people seeing the stone. I mean, look at the guards they are strapping young men who won't let anything happen. Besides, you're staying with the procession, aren't you?' Lindany nodded and smiled.

'For once Zyman was out-voted, I'm not the only one who wants to make sure this goes without a hitch. I realise old water-boy, Oroch, and others are only worried that they will be stuck for another fifty years working the elements, but I can understand their point. There comes a time when retirement has a strong pull.' For a moment, both Walkers stood in thought about what was going to happen, but soon shook off the feeling and regained the air of power that people knew and trusted. Without discussing the plans, Lindany motioned for the trailer, created for the stone, to be pulled up toward the metallic side of the wall. It looked almost like a four-poster bed on wheels. A thick veil, which would be draped around the stone, was tied to the corner posts.

With guards on hand to calm the horses and monitor the surroundings, the Walkers began the process of moving the stone. The ripple in the side of the metal began to form a portal through to the chamber within, its hazy edges merging with the grey of metal causing it to look almost misty. Makkan spoke with total authority.

'Look to your duties and do not look to this stone.' He waited only a moment before he slowly began to build up the wind speed around the DragonSoul Stone. Almost as if it was on a cushion, the stone began to rise. The stone itself was vast - as large as a boulder - but perfectly smooth. The golden tint to its surface almost seemed to ripple as the light shimmered from within, flicked about its surface. The movement was slow but, as if directing a feather, the Air Walker raised the stone through the portal and rested it upon the trailer. Once it was placed securely in the centre of the trailer, another flourish of air pulled the drapes shut all around, and the stone was once again concealed. From above the roof of the trailer, you could see the light rippling into the air, and on the odd occasion, a sudden shaft of light would flash from the bottom of the trailer. Both Walkers looked to each other and nodded.

'Tell Zyman the procession is starting.' These words were the last thing Makkan heard, as he stepped back into the portal to the castle. The guards took their positions around the 'float' and the procession got underway.

'I'm so fed up of waiting! I just want this bit over with!' Eric's tone was quite caustic as he sat to the side of the council chamber with the other Royals. Tanya and Johan were sat to one side of Eric and frowned at him as he said it, but Simon and Liam agreed. Simon moved some of his mopped dark hair away from his eyes with a flick of his chin and sighed.

'Perhaps old Makkan got lost on the way!' he chuckled at his own joke and though Liam laughed he added 'funny, but now isn't the time. Glasgow knows we don't want his wrath going off again eh?' all slowly nodded to that sobering reminder.

'Yes, and that will be us...' mumbled Eric. John was about to make a comment when the doors to the

DragonWalkers' council chamber began to open. As the doors opened, the Royals rose to their feet. Tanya was last one to stand. Her nerves had got the better of her and her legs had taken a moment to work. They turned as one to face the door and were greeted by the sight of someone who looked so regal, yet wore clothes happily seen in the market. This was Zyman, the Natural Walker and leader of the first generation of Walkers.

'Welcome. Please, enter the chamber....'

Milli could not be happier with her vantage point for the festivities - once she had managed to drag her eyes away from the uniqueness of the inn. It had been amazing to sit and watch the passers-by as people began to take their places along the main track sides, snaking their way up to the castle. Some had tried to stand on the castles edge, but they had soon been turned away. Ray seemed to have marked out a prize spot and her family, along with several other families from the metallic hold, all huddled together to get an unobstructed view. To Milli's keen eye the different styles looked juxtaposed with the metallic families intermingled with the wilders. The metallic holds had their grey, blue, black, red colour combinations of suits, smart dresses and denim, while the predominant colours of the inhabitants of the wilds were green, brown, yellow and the odd purple on cloth. The biggest difference was that all from the holds were holding up phones to take pictures, turning to take selfies and using other recording devices whereas the wilders were stood waiting and talking to a neighbour or simply clapping hands together and smiling, bobbing up and down on the balls of their feet in excitement. All the 'warm-up' entertainment, which had been spectacular, had come to an end. The music had stopped, the jugglers had left the road and all manner of sales carts had left the way clear. Slowly, like a Mexican wave, the roar of clapping and cheering seemed to ripple towards where Milli stood. She had jumped a couple of times to see over her father's shoulder before squirming her way to the front. She felt just like a child as she did that, but right now she didn't care - she could see down the road. The float made a slow procession down the winding road, led by Lindany dressed all in purple and looking like he was wandering up a street looking for shops. Looking away from the Walker, Milli caught sight of the float, which looked like an old four-poster bed - the shimmering light from within seeming to escape from any crack it could. She had read how it couldn't be touched, but she didn't know it couldn't be looked at. The float grew ever closer with the crowd cheering it on its way. As it was almost upon them, Milli noticed that every other person around her was taking pictures and selfies and she realised that that was a good idea. Not thinking about asking her parents to help, Milli turned her back on the parade, raised her phone into the air and took a picture of herself and the float.

At that very moment, several things happened that caught everybody off guard. Leaning back just a little too far, and not seeing the other foot, Milli stepped back and slipped from the kerb. She let out a high-pitched 'Oh!!' as her phone went one way and she went another. The cry, and being hit by a flying phone, had startled the horse nearest to her and it reared into the air, pulling part of the float up with it. Guards scattered one way; Milli fell another way.

The arm that had been raised to take the selfie helped to spin her round so her hands went out to try and protect her front and face. One hand hit the track, the other the inside of the float, her shoulder hit the cobble, her head scraping on the side. Lindany and the guards from her side of the float were still trying to calm the horse and keep the onlookers safe. Sweat and spit from the beasts was going everywhere, people from all areas were trying to see what was going on and the guards from the other side were succeeding in keeping the float as still as possible... but the inn keeper and her father were trying to help Milli up before she got crushed by the wheels. Trying to pull herself up, Milli reached into the float further, looking for anything to grip to help with leverage. Her hands found the cushion the stone sat on and just for the briefest of moments and with the most featherlight touch, a single finger brushed the surface of the stone, the contact so slight her mind didn't register that it had happened, but as she finally got up, her eyes passed over the tiniest gap in the curtain and glimpsed the stone within. She froze for a moment. The realisation that she had looked at the stone made her panic and she fumbled quicker to get up. ‘Help me up, help me up!’ she called as she clung to her father.

‘It’s ok, you’re up. It was only a little slip, no harm done so don’t panic. You’re not used to such uneven surfaces. Just take your time and let’s get you a seat.’ As Milli was led into the inn, Lindany called for the procession to start again, completely unaware that the stone had been touched and seen.

# Chapter 6

# The Birth of a New Generation

The commotion within the procession was soon forgotten, and the DragonSoul continued its journey towards the castle; the cheers from the crowed picked up pace once more. The atmosphere was too electric for what looked like a small stumble and fall to dampen any spirits. It slipped into the back of everybody's mind and celebrations continued; the only part being remembered was the antics of the horses and guards around the float. Milli tried to get back into the swing of the day by taking more pictures of the surrounding area, the people, the market and the very unusual inn, but her head was painful from the fall, and she felt her vision wasn't too good and voices seemed to grate.

The DragonWalkers now stood in two arcs with the glowing stone at their centre. It had passed through the walls of the castle the same way it had left the vault and now stood proud, glistening on its pedestal. You could cut the atmosphere with a knife. The old generation anxious, excited and worried about what was to happen to them. The new generation feeling the same for completely different reasons. Zyman had welcomed the Royals into the hall with the grace of someone who had accepted the passing of power. They had entered the great council hall with awe on their faces, along with apprehension showing through in their twitches, sweaty palms and people clearing their throat regularly.

'Welcome to you, the new generation to feel the balance and carry on the wisdom of our dragon kin.' Zyman's tone was soft and calming. His outstretched hand guided them to stand on the opposite side of the stone to the

DragonWalkers. 'From this moment onwards, you will hold the mantle of DragonWalker; we give you our souls freely and pass on our names with love and affection.' His head nodded towards the line of Walkers spanning away from him around the DragonSoul Stone. 'From now on we will accept our human names and you will become whoever chooses you. Take their names with pride. Never forget your roots, your home, your people, but work together for the good of all. Each of you has worked hard on your studies, and Makkan speaks highly of you all and he is a tough task master.' There was a note of fondness in his voice for their guiding tutor.

The intensity of the shimmer from the stone began to pulse, and Zyman nodded to all in the room. Raising his voice slightly, he smiled.

'It is time. Step forward and place your hand upon the stone.' Everyone in the room did as he was bid, and almost all in the room closed their eyes. Only Eric and Simon were glancing around to see what everyone else was doing. But surprisingly, nothing happened. For a long time, all stood as still as the stone itself. Slowly the candidates began to open their eyes and frown.

'Well?' Commented Makkan, directing this question to Zyman, who gave a slight shrug. The atmosphere was broken as Eric patted the DragonSoul Stone a few times and sighed.

'Were we supposed to say something? Chant something? Did you old guys forget something?' The scowls he got from everyone showed this was not the time for joking, but Eric didn't seem to notice and patted the stone again. After a few moments, Zyman gave the order to all take their hands from the stone and stand back into their respective semicircles.

'Perhaps we should use some of our Magi….' His sentence was cut off by a blast of light that seemed to ripple outwards from the stone, like the rings of Saturn, and rocked everyone back on their heels. After the initial blast, the shimmer of light focused from the top of the stone up into the ceiling of the castle and beyond. It opened out like a vast projector beam, and the ceiling of the council chamber shimmered out of existence. Rising within the arc of light grew a giant dragon – its body created by mist, its outline rippling with energy as though it was the sun being eclipsed by the moon. The radiating energy was hard to look at, yet nobody could take their eyes of it. It slowly unfurled great wings as it arched its powerful neck. The mist of its scales solidified just enough to give it substance. The majestic dragon hung in the air with its wings beating in a lazy back and forth motion, its tail flicking slightly at the tip.

Anyone who was standing, sitting, walking, riding in Warwick suddenly stopped and turned to the sky as one by one they became aware of the dragon. Milli and her family had begun the journey back to their car, in the same trailer as before, and though Milli had not really wanted to leave, her mother had the meeting she warned her about. Milli's eyes grew wide as the dragon-form seemed to be sweeping the sky with its great head. She raised trembling hands to take a photograph before making sure her family had seen the dragon too. She kept looking up as long as she could, but after a while her shoulder began to hurt, and she had no choice but to turn her head down towards the ground. The dragon hung in the air silently before its great maw turned downwards, its sinuous neck swaying left and right in time with its silently beating wings. All got the impression that it did not really need to move its wings for this flight, but it was doing so out of a habit from life. Its four clawed feet pawed the air with its spines seeming to pulse in time with its breathing. Fear started to grip the young Royals and a couple of them stepped back. Tanya's legs, which had been unstable from the start, buckled and she fell to her knees, while the older generation all seemed to be placing their hands on their hearts, or their heads, or raising them towards the figure. Finally, it spoke words, direct into the minds of both the Walkers and Royals below.

'*My children. You have worked hard, you have helped the mankind of England to keep the balance. Your magic flow has stayed positive and I feel your love for these people.*' As if given the command to do so, all the

DragonWalkers slowly sat down and crossed their legs, subconsciously understanding that this called for a state of meditation to allow the DragonSouls to commune. In their minds they all saw their dragon counterparts sit back on their haunches, open their wings and raise their necks to the sky. The noise that then came from the dragon of mist was almost a purr.

'*Are you ready to begin your duty once more? Will you continue to take the balance until mankind and magic are one again?*' Each dream state dragon-form bowed their head and hummed the words

'I will'.

Though the Royals had no idea what was going on, they all kept quiet. As if the 'I will' was an acceptance, the dragon of mist turned to the Royals and its golden eyes seemed to bore into each one, though he looked at them as a group.

'*My kin have accepted their responsibility. Do you?*' His tone was deep, like the depths of the ocean washing over them. Some trembling, a couple with tears in their eyes, they all slowly bowed their heads and echoed the dragonkin's words.

'I do.'

The waves of his voice battered them as he made sure all were aware of the trust his kind was putting in the next generation. The misty dragon shifted slightly into a more solid form as he seemed to be slowly taking more life from the stone.

'*You are fledglings - just a speck in our lifetime - but you need to learn, you need to understand the gift and the responsibility you are about to hold. My soul is encased in this stone, to enable me to guide my kin. My responsibility to you now is that I will take on the elements. My power is vast, and I will hold all, but I can only do this for a fleeting time: a time long enough for the transition to take place and for you to become one with my kin. As each of you takes on the mantle, I will pass the responsibility back to you. I do not wish to hold it for myself, allow me to assure you of that. I have neither the want nor the energy left for such a task. But allow me to do this now*'. His body seemed to entwine itself about the castle's turrets as he closed his eyes and opened his maw as if to roar. No sound came out, but each of the older DragonWalkers slowly slipped into unconsciousness. Some slipped out of their sitting position with grace to a sleeping position; others fell backwards.

'I'm not sure…. I don't think I can do this...' whispered Tanya as she watched her mentor seeming to grip his chest before falling the last distance to the floor.

'*My childling, I see the strength in you. I feel your heart. Have faith in yourself.'* The dragon of mist seemed to be trying to speak in a softer voice just to her, but it still took all her control not to cry out at the touch. Suddenly Liam pointed to where the DragonWalkers lay

'My faith!' he called, and all looked over to the other semicircle.

Like ghosts rising from the dead, shadows were forming above the still bodies of the Walkers. The draconic shadows had no substance but held slight colouration which marked them as their elemental power. They rose from the bodies with wings outstretched, their back legs looking slightly elongated as if they had taken on part of the human characteristics. Their arms were down by their side with their hands turned inwards, like a human, ending with glistening claws. Their tails swept the floor before turning up at the ends as if to keep them from touching anything. While the group watched, the souls stretched and began to walk forwards, some dropping into their natural four-legged form, others continuing to stride upright. The Royals were frozen, each one unable to take their eyes off the scene before them. The shadows walked away from the bodies they had just left. Out of the corner of his eye, John noted that the grey shadow of the air soul looked back at Makkan and seemed to almost turn back - its maw opening and closing as if to call to his human, and its eyes looking sad. It turned away and walked towards Tanya. She stood facing the draconic form with eyes bulging.

'*You have been chosen first my childling. Accept this gift and become Makkan.*' Tanya finally remembered her training and placed her hands on her heart.

'With heart and soul' She said the words only with a trembling whisper but that was enough. The shadow passed over her and she closed her eyes and drifted into unconsciousness.

A few other souls went directly to different individuals. Liam accepted and became Lindany. As with Tanya, he lowered himself to his knees as his eyes drooped and closed. John knew the honour he had been given as the soul of Zyman walked towards him with the power of a leader. Eric glanced towards John and frowned for a moment. Then Eric watched as the second Natural DragonSoul, Yebby, walked towards him. Eric smirked as the natural soul stood before him. While he voiced the words

'heart and soul' - his mind had already become heady with the fact he would have the power of all elements and would be the leader of the team. His mind closing off from the soul, he began to picture how he would look using his power. He closed his eyes and felt the soul begin to merge, but as though his thoughts had placed a barrier to the DragonSoul, suddenly it was gone. Eric opened his eyes and looked around him. At the same time as he realised that he had not received a soul, the great dragon who had begun to hold the balance seemed to belch plumes of smoke which would have once been fire, - its purr turning rapidly into a growl. Eric was lost for words.

He looked about him at all his colleagues who were unconscious on the floor.

'What just happened?' He went over to a couple of different people trying to get a response. 'Simon?' Tapping his shoulder lightly with his foot, but he did not move. Going over to John he did the same. 'Wake up.' While Eric was continuing to try and get a reaction of some kind out of someone, the dragon's grumbles must have stirred some of the old Walkers who began to moan. Eric went straight over to the one who used to be Zyman. 'Wake up. Tell me what's happened?' The gentleman opened his eyes and looked round for a moment before Eric knelt in front of him and shook his shoulder slightly. 'Where is my…' he stopped mid-sentence as he registered the old Walker's eyes. They were both human now, but he had one blue and one green. One had kept the colour of his dragon, an honorific mark. He had no time to dwell on this and shook him again. 'Look, what happened? where is my soul?' The old Walker was about to try and answer, with a mouth feeling parched, when the Walker who had been Makkan seemed to groan and was still clutching his heart, as he had before.

'I'm Steve…Alan?' Steve pointed for Eric to go over to the old Air Walker. Eric did as he was asked but he didn't help him.

'Alan is it? Alan, you were our mentor. What has happened? Where is my soul. By faith I need an answer.' He shook him slightly on the shoulder as his urgency was growing. Alan didn't answer but groaned in pain. Eric did not seem to notice the signs of pain, as his mind was in such turmoil. He dropped Alan back to the floor and went back to the old leader. 'Tell me?' Steve's eyes were widening as he watched the actions of the young Royal.

'What have you done… where is the soul?' Eric straightened up then and shouted at the dragon of mist for answers. The distressed beast did not answer but all were aware of subtle changes around the castle. The air was growing heavy, storm clouds beginning to form in a swirl above the castle's turrets. Suddenly, a window to the side of them smashed, and vines began to creep their way in, that had clawed their way around the castle walls. A second window shattered in the same way as they realised that the dragon was slowly turning its magic to the negative, in the distress of losing one of his kin. Sand and soil around the castle were beginning to form into sandstorms that were battering its walls. The vines that had entered the building were withering and beginning to decay in front of their very eyes. The wind storms were building in speed, and in the distance they caught the sound of screams, and they realised all who had been watching now saw the castle being attacked.

'What have you done…' groaned Steve, as he began crawling his way towards Alan, who had turned very pale, his lips blue and his hand almost clawing into his chest. 'Please...' Steve tried to say to the dragon, to Eric, to someone, but his voice was lost as a quake rocked the very foundations of the castle.

Eric began to back away from the image before him of all his fellow Royals, now Walkers, lying unconscious on a floor being rocked by the foundations; decayed vines clawed towards their still bodies, the older generation struggling to wake, with Steve reaching out to Alan. Eric couldn't take it. He backed away from the scene before him, shaking his head in denial from all that was happening, his only remaining thought being that he needed to find his soul.

Steve was beginning to panic as he had no idea what to do. He felt whole but weak, and with no power at his disposal he could not think of a way of calming the great beast. In all his years he had held the balance, and now his worst fears were being realised. He was just building the courage to try and call to the angered dragon when the grumblings turned to a slight keening, the keening to a purr, and the raging elements calmed. Though it did not retract any of the vines, the decay seemed to heal, the sand storms dropped to the ground and the sky cleared. There were a few more notes of keening before the great dragon lowered himself down onto the turret once more and seemed to be looking into the distance.

Steve gave himself a moment to wonder what had happened. His eyes scanned the unconscious Royals noting that a few had begun to get the colouration of scales around the draconic eyes. The speed that this was happening made him feel pride for Makkan's students. That thought brought him back to his friend. Steve crawled the last few paces to reach his friend and looked down into his face.

'Alan. Alan, they are all making strong bonds with their dragon souls. You should see it.' His friend slowly opened eyes that were bloodshot with pain and he coughed slightly.

'I am proud. They are fine young people.' His own miscoloured eyes looked into his friend's. 'We did well, we did it. The next generation can protect the balance…'

Steve nodded and smiled. He had managed to position himself so that he was now holding his friend in his arms. One arm supported his friends head; the other rested upon his friend's hands, which he still held to his chest.

'We did, you wind bag, we did it.' His friend coughed as he smiled at the fond nickname he had been given.

‘I am happy.’ With that final word his heart gave one last beat, and he let out his last breath. Steve cradled Alan’s head for a little longer, tears forming as he slowly closed his friend’s eyes.

‘Good night Air Walker’ was all he could think to say as the grief flooded over him. A hand rested on Steve’s shoulder as the gentleman previously known as Lindany realised what had happened. Steve nodded.

‘He gave his all. He worked hard to the end. Rest Alan.’

Milli was trying not to be sick from all the jolting around and could not help feeling the fear rising with what was happening at Warwick Castle. Her father asked the riders to pick up the pace towards the car park.

‘My faith, what has happened?’ the guide rider asked, not arguing at all about picking up the pace as he pushed the horses into a canter. The cries from people around them showed that others were trying to leave, or at least trying to get to some sort of safety. Tony was very worried about Milli as this had been her special day, and if everything was alright. He was strongly aware that she seemed to drift into sleep or was complaining that her head and shoulder hurt. He must get her checked over once back home. He watched as she slowly seemed to slip into sleep again, but this time he thought she mumbled

'heart and soul' as she slipped into unconsciousness. Milli's parents looked at each other with concern in their eyes; was that something they needed to report?

# Chapter 7
# Twisted Fate

Zyman stood facing a small reflective glass, situated in his private rooms. Below the glass, his hands rested on the rim of his sink. It was taking some of his weight as he leaned forward to peer closer into the glass. His eyes stared at the reflection before him, which he was slowly coming to terms with; externally the changes were striking. Since morphing from John and taking on the mantle of the Natural DragonWalker, his remaining slate grey eye definitely looked darker around his slightly enlarged pupil, with the white of his eye clear and crisp. His other eye now looked back at him with the deep green lizard iris. The slit pupil also slightly widened to take in as much light as possible from the room. Surrounding the draconic eye were a few scales that had slowly appeared since the transition of souls. They glistened like fish scales, with iridescent shades of green: Zyman's true colour. He blinked and watched as both eyes echoed the motion. Smiling at his reflection, his eyes were drawn to his teeth; he could have sworn his canine teeth has elongated just a little, but he wasn't sure. His hair looked less coiffed than before he became a Walker, and fell with a little more disarray, but other than that he looked ready for the day ahead. He mused that he was so different but still, in essence, John. Nodding once to affirm he was ready, Zyman stepped away from the mirror. He absently checked his clothing while his mind wandered over all that had happened since he woke on the council room floor.

The shock of Alan, once his tutor, passing was hard to swallow, but that was nothing compared to the misfortune that had befallen his twin brother. His mind turned to Eric, and he felt his DragonSoul giving emotions of comfort. Zyman had been lucky; From the moment their souls had entwined, and his meditation had allowed him to commune with his DragonSoul, he had felt at peace within himself and as one with the dragon. They had spoken much in his mind, but now while he was awake and focused on the day his dragon was still there supporting him by pushing to the fore the emotions that it felt.

'I can't keep doing this. We need to work out what has happened to Yebby. We need that second Natural DragonSoul. The balance is now ours to protect, but with Oroch (Darryn) and Makkan (Tanya) struggling, I can't keep this up! We need...' Zyman was not sure what they needed. He let out a breath and the dragonic soul seemed to thrum inside his mind, accepting his concern but giving him the support, it could. Zyman shook his head, straightened his shoulders and left his room, heading towards the council chamber.

Over the days that had passed since the DragonSoul procession had been completed, the Dragon of Mist has stayed above Warwick Castle, guiding the elements. During this time, everyone was aware that, day by day, it appeared to shrink, its essence reduced along with its effectiveness. It had been hard to watch, but all gave thanks to its support and guidance. There had been no further outbreaks of negative energy, but neither had it communicated verbally with any of the Walkers nor the older generation. As each Walker had become one with their preordained DragonSoul, the Mist Dragon relinquished responsibility of their elements back to them, and they had taken up the mantle of keeping the balance. Most were now relaxed and becoming more skilled, but Zyman still needed to be on hand to help. This was part of the problem and why he was feeling so uptight. He needed to help his brother, he needed to work out what happened; he needed to do many things - but they would all have to wait.

On entering the council chamber, Oroch, Makkan and Lindany were standing to one side. They had been working to help with the balance, but it hadn't gone too well. To the inexperienced group, the elements felt almost unstable, as though they could surge with power and strike the land or possibly slip away to nothing. It was not a comfortable feeling. It had been described as trying to hold two glasses of water level while riding a unicycle. The fear of what could happen if they lost the balance (dropped the glass) made the pressure even more intense. On this occasion, the remaining DragonWalkers had to take over. The three stood to one side looking quite dejected. Zyman smiled and nodded to all as he entered the hall. Looking at Makkan he spoke in a relaxed voice, avoiding adding further pressure.

'Tanya...sorry, Makkan, I have been thinking about what your problem might be. I have a task for you that might help - in fact it is for you, Oroch and Lindany. You are both going to be working with Makkan on this one.' The three looked at him expectantly and waited. Gathering his thoughts for a moment, Zyman nodded. 'You might not have seen, or remember, but when the DragonSoul of Makkan left his old soul companion, he looked back. I think he was the only one to look back and maybe he felt his friend's pain. Whatever we thought of our tutor, that look spoke a thousand words. Your soul possibly feels great loss for his friend as well as the fact that his passing could possibly be the cause of Alan's heart failure.' Tanya suddenly wrapped her arms around herself as a shiver ran down her spine. The feeling caught her breath, and it took a moment to get her breathing back under control. She was shaking as Zyman continued to speak.

'Sooth him Tanya. Support him. Reassure him that it was not his fault and that his friend loved him.' All waited for a moment while Makkan calmed. 'I apologise, Makkan. I called you Tanya. It's a habit I am going to have to break.' Oroch chuckled and nodded.

'We all are!!'

Zyman rolled his shoulders, running fingers through his hair making it more dishevelled.

'Now you see, this is what I think part of the problem is. Your nervousness impacted by your souls' grief. You need to build your bonds and respect for each other.' He turned to Lindany. 'Your bond is strong and steady, so I would like you to go with Oroch and Makkan. It was not just the wilds of Warwickshire that were hit by the power of the

Mist Dragon's anger, several other wilds have contacted us with blocked water supplies, fallen buildings and other such issues. His power with the elements was vast! I have never known a DragonWalker to be able to influence elements outside of their immediate surroundings, but he could! Imagine what he could have done if he were still living. Perhaps that is the true difference between DragonWalkers and Dragons?!' He paused to add focus to what he was saying. Continuing Zyman's eyes slowly went to each of the three before him. 'As both a diplomatic mission to show our support and to give you time to work on your bonds and skills, I'd like you to take portals to each affected area and help rebuild. If you require any of the other skills along the way, Lindany can contact me. If we need you for any reason, I will be in touch. Is this something you feel you could do??' tilting his head to one side, Zyman looked both supportive and goading. The four stood for a moment looking at each other with their mismatched eyes and then agreed. As one they left the council, chamber and Zyman hoped he had done the right thing.

Zyman then walked to the centre of the room and closed his eyes. His mind's eye filled with the draconic form. The dragon sat in a space void of any other images: the space in his mind showing an empty grey floor and misty surroundings. The dragon appeared to be curled around itself in an almost feline way, it's tail twitching indicating its alertness. It opened its eyes and slowly raised its head. Blinking in a way that Zyman felt showed understanding, he asked in his mind.

'Are you sure about this?' The dragon huffed slightly and began to slowly unfurl.

'*I am. We are strong. We can do this.*' After a moment, Zyman drew himself back from his mind, drawing himself out of the meditative state and coming back to the space around him. Zyman opened his eyes and refocused on the room, but as he was coming out of his meditative state, he had mumbled 'for how long'. Shaking off the fear, he called to the four Walkers holding the balance in the room.

'Thank you, you are doing a good job. As we agreed: you four are going to hold the balance while the others work on honing their skills. Now both pairs of Earth and Fire

Walkers are strong so you two can swap teams as you need. As for you…' Zyman turned to look at the remaining Water and Air Walker '…Oroch and Makkan have taken on the request I had for them, so I am going to stand in and work with you. We will swap teams as needed.' The group about him paused and a few began to protest, but once again Zyman calmed the group by raising his hand, smiling calmly. 'It is settled, and I have discussed this with my soul. It is ok, we can do this.' A single nod was the response he got as the four that had been working stepped aside and began to relax from their duty. The last thing heard as the group left the council room was someone noting how tired John/Zyman looked.

Milan, once known as Simon, had stood to the side of the council chamber and watched all that had unfolded. Once he was sure that Zyman and the others were focused on the task at hand, he had turned his back and walked out, heading towards the library. He was sure he would find Eric buried in books there. Milan was the second of the Purple Walkers and now held the power of the portals, like his brother. It had surprised him that he and his brother had both been given the same skills, though he had to admit he was not as proficient yet as his brother, Liam, had become when he became Lindany. This was his thought process as he wandered through the corridors of Warwick Castle. A few people stopped to pay their respects with a bow, but he didn't pay any heed to this, so focused was he on his own thoughts. The passageways gradually became darker as he entered the older parts of the castle, and Milan soon found himself outside the library.

On entering, Milan saw a lone figure sitting at a table with a single lantern throwing shadows around the table. He walked over quietly before clearing his throat. 'Any luck Eric?' he asked by way of a greeting. The twin with the temper and spiked hair looked up with steel grey eyes and shook his head.

'Nothing. Those old fools said that all the knowledge to guide us would be left here, but nothing. The Natural Dragon's soul was right there in front of me. I felt it touch my mind and then it was gone.' Milan winced at the anger and pain he heard in his friend's voice, but he did not back away. Instead, he sat down, cupping his fingers together and resting them on the table.

'It has not been that long since the ceremony, and the fact that the dragon of the stone went back willingly still makes me think that the soul is ok somewhere; we just need to find it.' Eric slammed the book he was reading closed and looked accusingly at his fellow Royal.

'That's all well and good for you to sit there saying that - you have your soul!' he clenched his fists together and sighed. 'I did not mean to snap at you, I apologise. Yes, I know, patience! Everyone always goes on at me about patience, but this is so frustrating. I've looked in all the main sections I could think of and so far, nothing.' Both paused to look round for a moment before Eric leaned back into his chair and looked curiously at Milan. 'So, tell me. What's happened so far?' Milan raised one eyebrow then, without pausing, answered as honestly as he could.

'Most have become one with their souls and have begun taking on the balance. All Fire and Earth Walkers have become masters, but Oroch who was Darryn from Devon and Makkan who was Tanya from Truro are struggling, so

Zyman has sent them on a diplomatic errand to help them work on their skills. My brother Liam, now Lindany, has gone with them. John, I mean Zyman, sorry, is now working to cover for them but he looks tired and drawn. He needs to find the other natural soul as much as you do.' He looked slightly embarrassed at talking about Zyman with a respectful tone, but he had to admit he was doing an excellent job of leading. Milan continued. 'It wasn't just Warwick that suffered from the negative attack from the Mist Dragon, so he has sent the others off to help fix things. I don't know if anyone has spoken with the Metallic Hol....' Milan didn't get to finish his sentence as Eric suddenly stood up.

'That's it!! I will offer to go and speak with the holds. I will offer to help this way and ask for your help to get me there. That will take me away from both Zyman and my father's gaze and let them think that I am working my way to forgetting all that has happened...but in actual fact we can get to check the holds' internet and more importantly their vast stores of data and information. I can research this as much as needed without creating suspicion! Genius

Simo....Milan!!' The Purple Walker wasn't so sure they would find anything, but if it focused Eric and worked for him, he would see just how far this rabbit hole would go.

The days after the procession had been a little bit of a blur for Milli. Her headache had taken a few days to clear, and once the doctor had checked over her shoulder, she was given the all clear. She was still a little embarrassed because she felt that she had been far too ill from such a silly fall. The headache and blurred vision had not taken long to go, but the embarrassment of losing consciousness?! She hasn't remembered banging her head as much as she must have, but she did remember how silly it was to slip on a stone. She was also annoyed that because of the slip, her photo of the float was all blurred. Phone cameras were supposed to have an anti-shake system built in, but then she guessed throwing the phone and hitting a horse was more than just a shake. As soon as the family were home, on the evening of the parade, her mum had managed to get to her meeting with the Bristol fashion ladies and, by all accounts, had made some excellent sales, but her dad had got her settled into bed and called for the medical diagnostic kit. Often, when the diagnostic kit arrives, the automated system scans for your vitals and gives you a printout prognosis, but her father had asked for it to be escorted by a doctor, explaining that the accident had happened in the wilds. Milli noticed that her father seemed to make several calls that day repeating what had happened over and over. Once Milli had been given the all clear, it was obvious that the doctor wanted to hear all about the parade, and Milli was happy to oblige. She soon began to tire so the doctor had left. Nothing has been prescribed other than some rest, relaxation and some VR time out.

Milli had accepted this and put her thumb print on the diagnosis machine to prove she had consented to both the outcome of the visit and that she would follow the advice given. She then enjoyed a nice wander in Morla and a refreshing cup of mint tea. Taking off her VR equipment, she messaged her father to say she was going to bed and finally drifted off to sleep. This was the first night she noticed her dreams. They were all as random as ever:

swirls of colour leading her from green fields to rainbows in rivers; skyscrapers with no limit to their height. Just as she was slipping further into deep sleep, her mind's eye saw a dragon curled into the tightest ball, seeming to be trying to hide from the world. On seeing the dragon in such vivid clarity, Milli startled and woke. This was the pattern that Milli fell into over the next few nights. Each time the dragon would gain her focus and she would wake up with a start.

Eventually, as her temper was starting to get a little frayed through lack of sleep, Milli turned to the internet to try and find out some information. She did many searches, all along the lines of 'dragon sleeping in my dreams but I'm not sleeping'. As she expected, the amount of contradicting information was overwhelming, but she had the mind and focus for research so began to pore through all the information. Was it a premonition? Was it her mind's coping mechanism? Was it some sort of spiritual guide? So many ways of answering the same question. Her mind reeling, she closed the internet and flopped onto her bed. She must have been so wound up about the dragon in her dreams that as soon as she closed her eyes, she could see it. But this time its tail was twitching, and its eyes were glaring at her.

'Aaaaaa....' She woke herself up calling out and her mother was there like a shot.

'You're sweating!!' Mother and daughter wrapped their arms round each other, and Milli quietly sobbed.

John and Eric's father had been instrumental in getting the old generation of Walkers back to their respective homes. He had offered them room and support to live out the rest of their lives in Warwick, but all had declined the offer, explaining it was time to go home. He couldn't help but gaze into their oddly matched eyes, but he respected their decisions and organised guide riders to help them home.

'Steve, you and the other southern gentlemen have a long ride ahead of you; why not ask one of the portal Walkers?' the older man had sighed, his green eye shining slightly, giving all the answer the king needed as to why they couldn't go by dragon magic: the painful memories that might cause.

'I understand' was all he said before wishing him well and a safe journey. Only Alan (Makkan) had lost his life in the transition, but all felt the loss of their dragonic souls deeply. Steve had tried to explain to the king that it was like a fresh wound that needed time to heal, but like a sore it needed to heal from the inside first because if just covered and forgotten it would fester.

'I feel a lot stronger in myself then I think I have a right to at 68, and perhaps I have to thank our souls for that, but I have many years ahead of me and enough time to learn to fish and how to weave a basket!' the king chuckled at that, and with a fond smile and a hand on his shoulder he nodded.

'Get out of here, but know you are always welcome!!'

*Back on its pillar, all life seemed to have left the stone. No longer did it shimmer with all the colours of souls that had passed through - the gold smooth surface looking as lifeless as the stone it was. The walls of metal and stone were back in place, and the protective veil, no longer required, was left draped to one side of the float. The guards were minimal and already feeling the monotony of their job.*

# Chapter 8

# All Learn in their Own Way

After Oroch and Makkan had stepped through the portal, they watched Lindany pass through with the last of their supplies. Then, with eyes wide, they watched as the ripped edges slowly knitted back together and their view changed from Warwick to Exeter.

‘I tell you what Darryn ... um sorry ... Oroch that makes the journey back here so much easier than the ride we had to endure to get to Warwick!’ The tone of Makkan’s voice was heartfelt as her hand subconsciously rubbed her backside. The air in Exeter had a slight chill, with the sun slowly setting and the cloud formation covering what night sky could be seen. They had got all the equipment they needed to spend the night outside, but all would have preferred their first night to be in one of the inns. The group had agreed that they did not want any pomp, so camping would give them time to focus on what needed to be done and to plan, before heading towards Exeter Cathedral. The three slowly began to set up camp, working in silence and almost without thinking; they had all had a lot of practice setting up and putting down the camp site on the journey to Warwick Castle. It had been a luxury each time they had stopped in one of the metallic holds, but most of the time had been makeshift camps, or staring at the night sky from under single blankets. Lindany disappeared looking for firewood, while Oroch and Makkan set up the tent area.

They had managed to find a small clearing on the edge of a wood, with enough dense foliage that would enable them to hear anyone coming in from behind or to the side and to keep them concealed from any other travellers. In front of them was a small patch of open pasture, enough to give them some light and to free them from any feeling of claustrophobia. Looking to their left, through the smallest of gaps you could just catch a glint of the grey edges marking Bristol's hold; to the right would be Plymouth, but there were too many trees to see that horizon marker.

Oroch had just about placed the last large tree trunk around what would become the fire place, when a torrent of wind knocked him onto all fours. Looking up from that position he saw Makkan with her arms slightly raised from her side. They had not changed form, so he knew she was only lightly tapping into her magic, but she was using the air to stretch out the tent material. Once the tent fluttered into place and the corners were secured, she turned around to smile proudly at the achievement. Then she saw Oroch on all fours.

'What are you doing?' She frowned, looking down with hands on hips.

'You tell me! Next time you decide to use a little 'wind magic', check the direction of the back draft will you! I almost got gusted off my feet!' He slowly got himself up, brushing off soil and leaves from each knee as he stood.

'Gusted off?!' For whatever reason, the terminology made Makkan laugh, and soon the pair were chuckling at the incident. Lindany re-entered at that point, frowning about the laughter but too weighed down with wood to ask questions; plus, he was loath to admit he was struggling with their accent. Placing the pile of firewood in the centre, he looked round and admired the patch they had created for themselves.

'Shelter, cover, a view and a fire. You brought the lighters, right?' All three looked at each other and were soon laughing at the situation. So much for being prepared. Lindany shook his head, stood and slowly walked toward the woods; the only sign that he was going back to Warwick was the shimmer of light from the portal he had opened. Makkan and Oroch looked at each other and smiled.

'I now see what our tutor meant when he explained how important the Purple Walkers are. They sat down to wait for his return, and for a moment they looked at each other, both almost staring at the draconic iris of the other.

Oroch's was a clear crystal blue while Makkan's was a silvery white.

'They take some getting used to, don't they?' Makkan commented as she raised a hand to place it just under her eye. They both suddenly looked away from each other and fell silent and almost jumped when Lindany spoke.

'We have all gained that mark of honour from our souls.' For a brief moment the Purple Walker looked between Makkan and Oroch, with a strange expression on his face, before he crouched by the firewood and lit a nice blaze which they used to cook the broth they had brought with them.

'So tomorrow then,' Oroch started, 'Exeter got in contact to explain that they were having problems with flooding around the edge of the quay side. It's an enjoyed tourist spot for the more curious metallics as well as a relaxation area for the wilds so it has started to affect them. This one is going to be my focus. We will have to assess what is needed and go from there.' He paused to try and move his greasy hair but not much of it moved. He seemed thinner than before but with an aura of strength that had been growing over the past few weeks. He stood up suddenly, his face lighting up as if he had an idea. 'Get me the water carrier, will you?' Makkan obliged while Oroch closed his eyes and seemed to centre himself. After a moment, he shifted his position to a solid battle stance. He parted his feet, knees bent slightly and held his arms up either side of his shoulders. Bringing them together he slowly began to draw on the magic of water. His hands begun to change form as the claws extended and the scales shimmered across his now muscular arms. Both watched wide-eyed as the scales extended up his neck and slowly began to cover part of his face. Neither of them had seen this much of a transformation before, but as his upper torso seemed to become more draconic, so a swirl of colour was beginning to form between his hands. Moving his hands in and out slowly, he began to manipulate the space between them, drawing on the elements to pull moisture out of the air and into a bubble in front of him. Keeping the flow of magic steady, he raised his hands out in front of him, manipulating the water to move towards the water container. Once the carrier was full, he slowly lowered his hands and began to breathe deeply and calmly. The pull on the air around his hands faded and he opened his eyes. Both were clapping, and he smiled.

'We did it.' And he knew he spoke the truth, he could feel the emotions of pride running to him from his DragonSoul, making his cheeks flush. All bar the selective scales around his eyes had disappeared and his hands were back to normal. He sat down then and looked to his fellow Walkers. 'Cup of tea?' Both had nothing to say for a time and simply held out their travel mugs.

'You felt moisture in the evening air and brought water from it? That's a delicate touch!' They all discussed what had happened, and then the conversation went from one subject to another, which is how the three Walkers ended up spending an amicable evening together.

The next morning, their camp was made secure and the air, water and portal Walkers made their way to Exeter Cathedral, where they were going to be met by the Royal family in charge. Oroch had begun to get a little more agitated on the way. It had dawned on Makkan that this was Oroch's home wild. He would know people, and he would be seeing his family for the first time since the soul transition. He had been slowly hanging back but, with reassurance from his friends, he had kept his head held high and walked into the centre of Exeter looking as much the Walker as he was. On arriving in front of the great cathedral, all three Walkers had looked up toward its great stained-glass window and admired the workmanship that was still standing in 2167. It showed it's age in places but overall, the cathedral was as lovely as it had been before all the changes to people's lives. Most of the central shops still held some sort of business, but their look was no longer the sleek shop fronts but buildings with no glass, wooden extensions or cloth coverings protruding into the streets. They approached the front of the cathedral and called out towards the door. It was not long until someone came to the entrance. Lindany almost gaped as the lady looked the spitting image of Darryn, now Oroch.

'Mother!' he called, forgetting all graces and he hurried toward her with arms open. His mother's eyes opened wide and her hands went to her mouth.

'It's you!' she called, but sadly, her body language and facial expressions indicated this was not the loving greeting he had hoped for but more the respectful distance he was afraid of. Makkan saw what was happening and, without thinking, she walked up to the lady and embraced her, speaking in a warm tone:

'Kin, it is good to meet you. Sorry we came without fanfare, but we are here to help and did not wish to draw attention to ourselves. Oroch made us a cup of tea earlier, but I admit he is not the best... you wouldn't mind would you, before we get to work?' The flurry of emotions that Oroch felt towards Makkan almost burst out of his chest as his mother visibly relaxed and embraced him as a son once more. Tears were almost brought to his eyes by the embrace of someone who he had loved all his life and the growing respect and love he was gaining for Makkan. Stepping back from his mother, he smiled.

'Any English Breakfast?' They might be in the middle of the wilds, but their connections with the local holds had a few perks.

Over a pot of tea, Oroch's mother explained all the problems that they had been having at the quay with the water rising too high for the banks to hold, how much of the area had become waterlogged and how it was causing problems with deliveries, tourism and, more importantly, she was worried about it affecting the drinking water supplies to the wilds. She also related all the goings on that had been happening with his family before they then headed towards the quay. The three Walkers looked at the scene and discussed the situation allowing them to find a solution which they hoped would work. Discussing the plan with Oroch's family led to a few extra precautions being put in place. Runners were sent to request the aid of the local guards, while people worked with the local shop owners to close their doors, block their windows and vacate the area. Once all had been cleared from the area, the wild had an eerie feeling - the only sound being from the wind knocking on doors, sweeping at trees or rippling the surface of the flood waters.

Much of the plan relied on Oroch using a lot of energy, but, with the positive feelings around him, and with his draconic soul's approval, he knew they could do it. With serious expressions, Lindany moved the three from the quayside to a nearby bridge. He stood in the middle with Makkan on one side and Oroch on the other. They made a striking silhouette but that was nothing to what they were about to attempt. Nodding to each other, they focused their minds, feeling their draconic souls' support in tune with their own. Slowly, Lindany raised his hands, and a vast shimmering portal opened in the air; they could see the vast expanse of sea through the other side and knew he had found the right place. He slowly moved his feet so that they were in line with his hips, and he nodded.

'I am stable. Take your time and we can do this.' Both the others nodded and looked ahead of them. Makkan was the first to act, and all could feel the air pressure changing. Her hands already changed to that of her draconic form as her mouth was parted slightly in a grimace of concentration. The air current began to create a funnel - it looked as if it was coming out of the portal - to a wider opening above the flooded area. Now it was Oroch's time to help, and he began to slowly focus on all the flood water that was above the level of the quay. The surface of the water began to ripple, then churn and slowly began to rise, like a tidal wave, towards the air funnel - all the water slowly being siphoned off and dumped out into the ocean by the portal. It was working, and slowly, the levels began to subside. Though they knew Makkan could possibly have achieved a similar effect by sucking the water into the portal with her inverted tornado, she had worried that she would not be able to control it as well once water had begun to merge with it. Makkan and Lindany felt comfortable in their stance, and with the slight changes to their body they were stable and holding their position.

Oroch was the one that now had to step up his game to the next level. He had removed the flood water, but they planned to remove all the water from around the shop fronts, from the very wood that had been drenched, from each nook and cranny of the quay that had been water damaged. His mind and eyes were closed to all other senses bar his magical touch of water. Not realising what he was doing, his tongue flicked out, forked like a lizard to taste the moisture in the air. His legs had undergone a transformation that had everyone staring. His knees now buckled the wrong way, with strong thighs joining elongated calves. Feet now devoid of shoes showed talons the same as his hands. Ripping through his top in several places were spines that matched the colour of the deep ocean, opposite to that of his scaled body which shimmered a turquoise blue. His mouth, falling open as he panted with effort, showed canines visually extended. Never had he felt so in tune with the environment around him or with his draconic self. They were one and working in complete harmony. Was it him thinking or was it his draconic half? He could not answer, but they were doing it. All the water was being removed from the area, puddle by puddle; drop by drop.

As the last drops were cleared, Oroch spoke with a gruff voice to say it was finished. Makkan and Lindany lowered their arms and allowed their magic focus to ebb away. Oroch was still in tune with his dragon and had not opened his eyes or stopped his pull on the magic. Both Walkers stared at the man before them, who no longer looked human. Finally, he dropped onto all fours and began to take deep gulping breaths. As he did this, and his breathing calmed, he slipped back into the form of Darryn that they remembered. His greasy hair was still in place, and his thin form looked too thin as he stood up; but when they investigated his face, they both realised it was a different person who stood in front of them now. He was a true DragonWalker. His eyes shone, and he smiled broadly, speaking with a conviction that had never been there before. ‘We really did it!’

As Zyman sat within the council chamber, he felt such a strong pull on the waters elemental balance that he almost lost control. It rocked him where he sat, and as if the energy was being stolen from near him, he looked around for what had happened. The feeling had gone as quickly as it had started. And apart from frowning, he continued with his job and thought nothing more of it.

After bidding a fond farewell to Oroch’s mother, the three returned to their camp site. They had been offered a place at the inn for the night, along with many other gifts of thanks from all affected by the flood, but they politely declined and headed back to where they had been camped. They did take some nice tea bags with them, however, as they felt they all deserved a good cup of tea. The fire was lit once again, and after all the energy they had used, Lindany had nipped back to Warwickshire, reported to Zyman, and returned with some roasted pork to have with the remainder of their soup.

'What are you looking at, Makkan?' asked Oroch, once he had emptied his mouth of the delicious meats. She raised one eyebrow, tilting her head to one side and smiled - an action that made the colour rise in his cheeks.

'You can't see yourself, but you should.' He wiped a small bit of the five-spice grease from his chin and frowned.

'Why?' he looked from her to Lindany and back again. 'Why?' he asked again, but neither answered. Finally, Makkan went into her tent and returned with a mirror. He stared into the glass for a time before slowly looking at them both with a gaping mouth.

'My ears! My teeth!' They both nodded.

‘You should have seen your forked tongue earlier, thank faith that has gone back to normal.’ He looked back to the glass as his free hand raised up to his ears, which were now prominently pointed. His finger then ran down from his ear, over the protruding turquoise scales around his eye to his mouth, where he pulled his lip up slowly showing extended canines still in place.

‘I don’t get it. The old generation had no such alterations to their physical form, only their eye. What does this mean?’ All sat looking at him for a while, which made him squirm more before Lindany finally answered.

‘You said earlier, on our way back to camp, that you felt truly as one with your draconic soul while you focused on the task of removing all the water, yes? You have now worked in harmony like nobody has before. Yes, the older generation kept the balance and supported the wilds, but had they ever undertaken a task as you have today? Perhaps you have taken things to the next stage. I mean, you should have seen yourself! Your ruined shoes and shirt showed you just how much you transformed.’ Makkan leaned back and nodded.

'I noticed that Zyman's teeth were more canine in shape, and he has been working hard for days. He had a true joining of souls from the start, but maybe you have pushed yours further: Your acceptance and wanting to work well opening your mind and heart further?' This brought them to a whole new train of thought - one that made them all quiet while they finished their meal. The only noise came from Oroch as he continued to look at his ears and teeth from different angles.

Milli had got herself into an unhealthy cycle. It was slowly beginning to affect her ability to keep up with her studies. She would go through the motions of joining her friends, relaxing in MorlaVR or doing college work through her classroom-based avatar, but in the evenings, she would continue research until she finally fell asleep out of frustration and fatigue. There she would stand in a space seemingly devoid of all colour and substance - a grey space with nothing to separate floor from sky, apart from the small green dragon that was curled in the corner: sometimes looking at her, but often curled up and sleeping.

She would wake up with a start once she registered the beast was there and eventually either continue sitting in Morla to relax her body at least or sit on the edge of her bed watching the changes of colour in the night sky above Coventry. Her parents were showing more and more concern, but each time she was questioned, Milli just explained that she was fine, but she couldn't sleep. They would never take her on vacation to the wilds again if they knew about this repetitive dragon dream.

Finally, she decided that she needed to talk to someone about this. After a lot of deliberating Milli waited until her next college class, to speak with her professor. The group had spent the lesson at desks, taking notes on the different sections of the lymph system. The lecture had been interesting, but her anxiety had been growing throughout the session. As the class was dismissed and several of her girlfriends logged out, Milli moved over to the professor. The lady who was their lecturer looked at her and smiled.

'Milli, I am glad you have decided to speak to me about whatever is bothering you as I am concerned about your work levels.' Milli blinked a few times and looked surprised.

'Dr Bannerman, I... how did you know?' The Doctor tilted her head slightly and shrugged.

'Call it medical intuition. And yes, I have time to speak with you, I have been holding 10 minutes at the end of each session in my diary in case you chose to approach me. Now please sit and call me Pat.' It took Milli a moment to grasp what had just happened, but once she had, she settled into a seat and nodded.

'I. Well.' She didn't know where to start.

'Start at the beginning, as that's always the best place to start, unless you want to give me spoilers: then start at the end!'

'What... oh!!' Milli smiled then continued. 'On my 18th Birthday I had the best present of going to the wilds for the DragonSoul Stone procession… I was so in awe of the whole place...' Milli told the full story and left nothing out. She explained about falling, she explained about the headache, the medical report that she was fine and how, since then, she had begun seeing a dragon in her dreams, but now her mind was devoid of dreams and she always fell into the grey space where the dragon either slept or looked at her with the most amazing eyes. For a long while Pat was silent; she seemed to lean into her chair and fold her arms. She then asked about the research Milli had done and listened quietly regarding all the different possibilities that had been presented to her from the internet searches. Pat fell into silence again before leaning forward and staring into Milli's face. She breathed out almost in a sigh and then smiled.

'You have a fascination with the wilds that oozes out of your every pore. Why you were not chipped and tagged as a wilder I have no idea, but your aptitude and studies does work in your favour, within the metallic holds. I am wondering if this is your mind dealing with the conflict that you possibly have inside, now that you have experienced life in the wilds. You hear about it all the time: people who break down because they cannot cope with the world around them. Maybe this is your mind's way of coping? Perhaps the dragon is the manifestation of your 'wilder self', and it is waiting for you to consider what you want your future to be? Where you should be?' Pat stood up and went to her log in screen. 'Talk to it. I don't mean literally, but if this is your mind's way of getting your attention, then you need to focus on the problem head-on and deal with the issues that are coming to the fore.' The Doctor's avatar disappeared, and after a moment Milli logged out. With VR sensors removed, chores completed, Milli had a meal with her family before making the resolve that she would tackle this problem head-on and went to bed.

Unlike all the Royals at the ceremony, Milli had no training on how to meditate, how to commune with a DragonSoul and how to build the bond and the joining. Milli had never mediated in her life, had no idea how to relax her mind and above all had no idea that she was not just about to talk to a manifestation of her mind but to the soul of Yebby, the Natural dragon.

# Chapter 9

# Matters of the Mind

As Zyman sat in the council room with his fellow elemental workers, his mind relished the time of quiet. He felt calm, relaxed and that slowly, all was coming together well. Reports were coming in, from across the land, that problem after problem was being fixed as the trio on the diplomatic mission were working on all the damage caused by the negative energy. Warwick had settled into its normal way of life, but there had been a few surprising changes since the parade. He never would have thought that the new road would bring with it more access to traders who had struggled to bring their wares into the wild. The car park had become a delivery point, enabling track dwelling traders to pick up commodities from the superslab cars. This had cut costs for many. His mood was light when the council door opened and Lindany, Makkan and Oroch walked in. The difference in them hit Zyman as soon as they entered. They were comfortable with each other, they walked with confidence and he felt that the magic flowing from them matched his own in stability.

'May We?' Makkan asked politely while bowing to Zyman. At a single nod, he felt his control of the balance shift as Oroch and Makkan took on the mantle. The two Walkers smiled broadly at the success they felt for being able to do their part and in joining the Earth and Fire Walkers doing their job.

Lindany stood to the side with his arms folded, a light smile playing on his lips. A slight flick of his hair was the only motion as he waited for Zyman to walk over. The Natural Walker rolled his shoulders before turning to stand beside someone who was quickly becoming his friend.

Who'd have thought it, considering how Zyman had felt when he had watched Lindany and his brother enter the castle what seemed like an age ago.

'The missions were a success then?' the Purple Walker nodded and smiled.

'Yes. I already told you about Oroch in Exeter; that is something that needs to be discussed at some point. You noticed his ears, yes?' Zyman whipped his head round to look closely, the surprise on his face confirming he had not noticed - but then, how often do you look at someone's ears? The pair continued to watch the four who were focused on their elements' flow for a moment before Lindany continued. 'Yes, he did an amazing job, but so did Makkan. Truro's cathedral roofing problem took a little more thought, but with force of will and the pressure she could create, the materials we found moulded to the curvature of the roofing and the gap was sealed.' Clearing his throat, he added, 'I know it was not on our list, but with those two getting to see home, I took us back to mine and we spent some time with my family. They seemed surprised by my changes. After seeing Oroch, I don't think

I've changed at all!!' Zyman's expression indicated that he thought otherwise.

'Talking of someone who has changed. Have you spoken with Sim....Milan since you have been back?' Zyman queried.

'No. I've not seen much of him. I got the impression he was slightly annoyed that we got the same skills. I don't know why.'

'He is one Walker I have not really spoken to at all and I just hope he is well.' He was also worried about how much time Milan and Eric were spending shut away together. He knew he could call his fellow Walker to undertake a mission at any time, which would keep him working and focusing his magic, but he did not want his brother to lose the one connection he seemed to have made. This thought of his brother decided what he was going to do next. Clapping Lindany on the shoulder, Zyman left the council chamber.

'I'm going to take this opportunity to leave the chambers for a while.'

Calling at the kitchen for a quick piece of bread and butter, Zyman walked towards his brother's rooms while eating. He realised this was possibly not a look a Walker should portray when in public, but he wanted to see his brother urgently. Twisting and turning through the corridors, he finally reached his brother's rooms. They were, in essence, the same as his but placed in a different part of the castle. That had been his father's decision as he had wanted them to grow independently not as a twin unit. Still, the bond of twin brothers had always been there.

Zyman knocked on the door and, as he had always done, said

'wake up and get the door, I am not going to wait.' Eric opened the door and, leaning on the door frame with his hand holding the door slightly closed, he chuckled.

'What if I had a lover in here?' The traditional sibling banter made Zyman smile broadly, and the pair smiled at each other as Eric threw the door open to allow his brother in, but Eric didn't move. Eric's smile became fixed as his eyes focused on his brother's teeth.

'Making more changes are you eh?' He nodded his head and Zyman snapped his mouth shut and walked into Eric's room.

'I keep catching my lip on them so don't go thinking it a momentous change ... I eat a meal and look like something out of a vampire movie with blood running down my chin!!' the comedy actions he then pulled made his brother grin. Walking across Eric's room and through double doors to a small balcony, the pair leaned on the railings and looked at the view. The wilds spread out in front of them like a patchwork of browns, greens and blues. The brothers talked amicably about what their father had been doing, the affairs of the castle and, more importantly, the *affairs* of the castle. Some partnerships you could see coming a mile away, but even Zyman looked surprised that the head chef had become the partner of the guardian from Glasgow.

'All the other guardians left once the ceremony had finished, but he decided to stay. It wasn't until I saw Chef Jacob and him together that I understood why the guardian had stayed. Father is considering his transition of post now.’ Eric lightly asked how his fellow Royals were and listened politely while he was told about the balance and the missions.

Zyman had always been good at picking up his brother’s emotions, and something in the way he was listening was starting to put him on edge. He felt his anxiety rise and realised it was his draconic soul’s warning. He didn’t stop telling his brother the news, but he began to cut out a few details. He had never done that to his brother before, and it distressed him to have this doubt. Eric nodded and continued looking at the view.

‘Seems like it is going well but hard work; you look tired and sound exhausted. I am worried about you.’ Eric turned to face his brother and placed his hands on his shoulders. ‘I am meant to be helping you with this but I’m not. I don’t know what happened, but I am no help to you as I am. I have been thinking and talking to Milan. We have been through all the library books with no information presenting itself’. Eric spoke in a tone that they both knew was slightly fake. ‘I want to help you and I have had an idea that I’ve been meaning to run past you. It wasn’t important enough to disturb you. I would like to go to Coventry and access the metallic holds data network ... no, no, wait, I know what you are going to say: we have access in the room here - but it's slow and does not include the virtual space access. If our library holds nothing, the old generation have no idea and neither do the souls. I'm sure you've asked them?' At Zyman's shrug, Eric nodded and continued. 'Right, so it's the last place to look. You know I'm comfortable in the local holds and have people who can help. No, I don't want you to contact the governors, and I don't want any ceremony.' That was the final alarm bell for the Walker, and he realised he had to make a snap decision. He did not like it at all, but to deny his brother this could alienate him even more. Zyman realised that his brother had not accepted anything, and the lengths Eric had gone to, indicated that his studying had twisted into an obsession. Zyman couldn't blame him and was sympathetic, but that did not help alleviate his concern. Sighing, he nodded.

'Ok, fine. But Milan will go with you for ease of transport and protection. I hope no Walker ever has to use the negative to their powers but, if needs be, he can slice a portal through someone.' Eric clapped Zyman on the shoulder and, with more spring in his step, he called over his shoulder that he would sort things and be gone by tomorrow. Zyman dropped his hands to his sides before turning back to look at the view. Never had his brother left him alone in his room.

Ex-DragonWalker Steve had been on his journey back home from Warwick for a good while. He had enjoyed long stops as he took in views he had not seen for years and ales he had never sampled before! His guide was more than happy to point him in the direction of the recommended inns, and if he liked the ale, they stayed for two or three days. A few inn keepers served him until they caught sight of his mismatched human eyes, at which point they either called out about a possession or grovelled at being in his presence. He found this irritating so had brought an eye patch and placed it over his blue eye. For some reason, he just did not want to cover his green eye.

'How do I look?' he asked his guard (rapidly becoming his friend). He received a chuckle in response and took that as a positive.

'Ok brain, you and me!' were Milli's final words before she lay down ready for sleep. She had tried to follow the doctor's advice on thinking about her fears, but all it had helped to do was make her feel like she was a very rounded person - an individual who contributed to the metallic society but enjoyed the wilds. She felt no remorse, concern or guilt over this and even when talking to her mother about it, she had not felt any concern. So, it had been back to the drawing board, but this time Milli had decided to research 'calming the mind'. She had had a little fun to start with, putting in search queries like 'how to talk to dragons' and 'how to train your dragon'. She had been surprised with the answer she had got for 'what language do dragons speak' as people had made up languages over the years. While trying to speak the words fanatically, she had got on with the more serious search and came up with some breathing exercises to help her stay awake while dreaming. They had not worked for the past few nights as she had ended up so relaxed that she fell asleep, waking up the next morning with a start. This time though she was more prepared. She'd had a nice cup of tea, opened all her windows so there was a good flow of air and put on the most relaxing music she could find. Now she lay with her eyes closed, harp music flowing around her and taking steady breaths. As she felt herself falling asleep, she shook herself. This happened a couple of times, but on the third try her body jarred her wide awake, or so she thought - but really, she had finally reached a point where her mind was now working independently of her relaxed body.

Milli found herself in a space devoid of anything but the grey mist surfaces and some sort of light source as she could see clearly. She guessed her dreams could just be doing that. There in the corner was the dragon. Curled like a feline, Milli could see the slight tendrils of smoke from its snout as it slept. Normally, at this point, she would have woken up shouting but this time she felt in control of her thoughts. It was as though she was not in her body lying on the bed but stood in the space. She took a few steps toward the dragon to look at it more closely. Its underbelly seemed to be almost lime green, the coloration travelling up its neck, down to the underside of its tail and across the membrane of its wings. The rest of the dragon's body was more of a deep olive green - all coming to an end around a lightly yellowed muzzle and claws. Teeth stuck out either side of its elongated maw in no order or spacing. Running from the top of its snout and up over its eyes were two long feelers that gave it the impression of looking quite serious. About its muzzle were a few thick grey whiskers showing it was older than it looked.

Because Milli's eyes had been so focused on the beast, it took her a moment to realise that as she moved forward, the smoke had stopped rising, the tail perfectly still, as if it had turned to stone. 'Ok Milli. This is insane but it's doctor's orders.' These thoughts were in her mind as she took one more step forward and then sat down. The dragon hadn't attacked so she thought she best not tower over the beast. Sitting down, she stayed silent and just politely waited. Eventually, the dragon's eyes slowly opened. She took that as a cue and began speaking. 'Hello. My name is Milli. I live here on the 73rd floor in the metallic city of Coventry. I have lived here all my life, but my doctor thinks that since visiting the wilds I want to go back because you have been here ever since.' The words tumbled out of her mouth in a rush. The dragon blinked but she had no idea if it had been listening or even understood. She had an idea and tried a couple of the words from the 'dragon language', but she couldn't say them anyhow. Shaking her head to focus back on what she was doing, she continued to look at the dragon. 'I have seen you every night since the day I fell over during the parade.' Nothing, no reaction other than the draconic eyes watching her warily. 'Do you need anything? Is there something I should be doing?' It dawned on Milli that she was talking to herself more than the dragon. She fell into silence and her mind drifted. Slowly she began to panic. How could she wake herself up if she felt so awake now? The panic welled up, and she began to look around her frantically for something that might signify an exit. It was this panic that woke her up with a start.

Sitting up in bed and panting, Milli realised she was sweating. She gathered her thoughts and calmed herself down and then thought about the whole incident. Shaking her head, she decided to go to sleep properly and try again tomorrow. When she woke up in the morning, she felt her dreams had been strange, as though she was seeing them with more clarity but that she was watching them as an outsider. It unsettled her a little, but as the day's activities started this feeling disappeared. That evening she decided to try again, and this time she found that she'd slipped into the relaxed state required slightly quicker, which pleased her. Once again, the dragon was there, but this time it was already awake. Milli went through the entire process again: introducing herself and waiting. More waiting. This pattern happened for the next four days. It was frustrating her a little, but she also found that she was eager to try again and thinking of ways to do this started to fill her mind during the day. On the fifth evening Milli relaxed with ease. No music or ambient lighting was required for her to reach into her mind. As she stepped into the mist, she almost gasped. The dragon seemed to have grown somewhat and was sitting up. This threw her and for a moment she hesitated, but finally she took her normal sitting position. Without thinking, Milli spoke her thoughts.

'You sit just like a cat. I thought that about how you sleep too.'

'*How do you expect me to sit? This is comfortable for me.'* The dragon spoke back in a light voice. It sounded deep, but essentially feminine in tone. It blinked twice and Milli blinked back. It had spoken. It had used her language. Now what?!

'Oh, I am sorry, I meant no offence. I have never seen a dragon sitting, so my mind must be making you more feline.' She mused, but again the dragon shocked her by correcting her.

'*No, this is how I sit. I am comfortable.*' Silence … each looking at the other. How long the silence continued, Milli did not know, but without knowing when, she must have fallen deeply asleep because she woke up with a start back in her room with the morning light shining though her windows.

Over time, Milli and the dragon slowly felt more and more comfortable together, talking in such a way that any problems Milli had during the day would have a solution the following morning. Milli seemed to be doing most of the talking, but she got the impression that the dragon enjoyed their time together, and a bond of friendship was forming. On the latest visit to the grey mists, Milli had spent more time there than she had meant to and had woken suddenly. Looking at the time, she started to rush around and got herself focused and ready for College. Headset on, sensors in place, Milli was back in the VR College with just enough time to sit down before Doctor Bannerman came into the room. During the session one of her friends leaned over, smiling:

'We're doing another boss raid after this. You in?'

'I am sorry, I can't. I have a meeting booked with Dr Bannerman.'

‘Again? She kept you behind the other day; what’s going on? Damn it Milli, we need your healing skills. The raid leader is good, but we keep having to draft in other healers from different guilds, and you know how that usually goes…!’ Milli did; it normally went badly, but she couldn’t help it, her mind was already thinking of her next dream meeting. Her friend leaned back, turning to another colleague and shaking her head, the disappointment obvious on their faces but there was always tomorrow. The lesson finished, and all clapped their hands to remove the keyboards that were in front of them. The glass screens they had been entering statistics into were closed, and everyone began to log out one by one.

‘Dr Bannerman. May I?’ The tutor nodded and Milli approached.

‘You seem brighter today Milli. Have you made progress?’ Smiling broadly, she nodded.

‘Your advice has been so helpful. I have done so much thinking, and I feel I am whole, but the dragon of my psyche is still there, so we have been talking together.’

The doctor had not expected that, and for a moment she frowned.

'You are talking with your own mind, Milli; it is you who answers you; it is you who is trying to work out the problem. Remember, it is a manifestation of your own mind.'

Frowning and slightly perplexed by this, Milli nodded that she understood and with renewed apprehension she logged out. Letting her parents know that she felt well and had a good chat with her friends and tutor today reassured them. Telling them she was going to go into Virtual Reality so if she didn't answer messages it was because she was gaming, she slipped off to her room. It was normal for Milli to have evenings lasting a fair few hours when she was involved with the games she played. Of course, this was not what she was going to do, but she was soon lying on her bed and meditating into her mind.

Milli was not sure how much time had passed but this visit to the dragon of her mind had been very different. When she had sat down, the beast had risen onto all four feet, its wings slightly unfurled for balance as it walked around her, looking at her, smelling her, prodding her with its muzzle. Milli stayed perfectly still until it had finished its inspection.

'This does not make sense. The doctor explained that you are my mind and I am trying to work out what the problem is, but here you are looking at me. Am I making a bond with my own mind?!' The crossed wires which Milli was unaware of were soon to change her life for ever.

'*I am Yebby. You are you.*' The dragon huffed slightly. '*We want to be whole mind and soul. We want to be one.*' Yebby? My mind has a name?

'Yes, I don't want to be split'. She nodded, thinking this was her thinking finally coming together.

'*Do you care for people? Do you like nature*?'

'I do. I am training to be a nurse to care for people. I like flowers, plants, the fields. I loved the wilds'

'*You will stay open to me and not shut me out?*' This question came from how the DragonSoul had been treated when it had touched Eric's mind.

'I…I did not mean to shut you out in the first place. I didn't know I had.'

'*We will be together. We will be one heart and soul. You have spoken those words before.*' A slight memory stirred of her father telling her she had said that in the trailer in the wilds. She didn't really remember, but then it had seemed a pleasant thing to say. She nodded. The dragon hummed and raised back onto its haunches, spreading its magnificent wingspan as it opened its wings to trumpet into the air. Milli was in awe of the sight, reacting to the moment and, without realising what she was doing, stood and opened her arms wide, welcoming the beast.

# Chapter 10

# Reality Hits

Milan was sat to the side of a small hotel room, his body language and expression showing he was becoming bored with looking out of the window at the view of Coventry. Originally, the contrast of slate grey and glass towering to the skies, compared to the wilds, had kept him fascinated. Now he sat leafing through a courtesy magazine, explaining all that was going on for the week of your visit. He sighed and looked up. In front of him, sat on the bed, was Eric. Eric was plugged into a Virtual Reality headset and had been like that for what seemed like hours. Eric had caused quite a stir when he had booked the rooms days ago. Normally, any Royal visit would require announcement; however, on this occasion, they didn't want any such ceremony. Since the day they arrived, nobody had seen Eric enter or leave the room and Milan had followed once the door to the suite had been closed. Laundry outside the hotel room was the only sign that the room was in use. Having Milan to provide portals had been very helpful; plus, the pair did not really want to explain the Walkers appearance to anyone, least of all the Governors of Coventry. If they were to get wind of a Walker in the city, it would be a big pain. Milan slowly closed the magazine before slamming it down on the table. His hand remained on top of the magazine for a moment before he rose and walked over to the window, frowning.

'What are you trying to find, Eric? You have been at this for days…' He mumbled this to himself knowing he would not get an answer. At one point, the Royal had got quite excited as the algorithms from the search engines had shown that there had been quite a few searches on dragons, but the results had been dismissed as they had just been in connection to the parade. The pair had had quite a debate as Eric wondered if he could influence anyone to find out who had made those searches. Pointing out that current data privacy rules and regulations would not allow this information to be shared, Eric had changed tack and had been looking at news reports and various feeds ever since. The only thing that had been vaguely interesting was several reports that a girl had fallen during the parade and had to be helped from the floor, stopping the float. Pictures of her falling had become 'memes' over time, especially the part where the girl's phone had hit the horse. People had had great fun with that one, and the girl who fell must be so annoyed that it had gone viral. Still, the pair could not see any reason to pursue that link and had dismissed it as old news. Milan mumbled to himself again,

'I'm going to have to report back to Zyman soon...' He jumped and spun round as Eric answered him.

'And what are you going to say?' The Royal had a steely look in his eye, but Milan countered it with his own carefree expression.

'Same as last time. No luck but the vacation is doing you good!'

'Hmmmm…' Commented Eric, who's demeanour had begun to change. The frustration was probably getting to him, but he seemed more withdrawn from everything, and his obsession was beginning to make him paranoid. Milan remembered the conversation of the night before, which had made him feel uncomfortable as Eric had said 'Maybe Zyman knows what happened but, being my brother, he wants to stay leader and not have someone else on his turf?!' Tonight, though, Milan was ready for any negatives and shook his head.

'We can go anywhere you wish - we could look in the other wilds, the other holds; but for now, you need some actual rest and to take a bath!' Eric raised an eyebrow at Milan's outburst but conceded. As he walked into the bathroom, stripping as he went, he called for Milan to order them some food. The Walker did as requested without question.

It seemed an age since the last time Milli had seen the dragon in her mind. That final night seemed to have cleared her mind, and Yebby was no longer in the grey mist. She had woken each morning feeling refreshed, almost vibrant. She had felt relaxed, calm and able to take on the world. She logged into her game and could heal her raid group in a way that nobody could complain about, and after that, her college classes had gone without a hitch. She admitted she was glad that these things were in virtual reality because she was not sure when it had happened, but she had really smacked her eye, resulting in a dark bruise forming around it, with a not nice greenish tinge. Her mum had called for some poultices to draw out the bruising, and with the speed that the bruise was turning green, the whole family felt this was working well. Milli had wondered for a time about the odd expressions on her parents faces: she wouldn't call it worry, - more concern, if there was a difference. She had not really dwelt on their expressions and, as Milli felt no pain, the bruising did not concern her. Her thoughts on her parents' odd expressions slipped from her mind as soon as she thought them. Milli had informed her tutor that the dragon of her dreams was gone, and she felt well. This comment had caused the hitch that now made Milli very nervous. Their tutor had informed them that now that the whole group was at the same point in their studies, they would be going into a live hospital for their next level of training and would begin putting theory into practice. Their shifts would be working alongside already-qualified neuro nurses. This was what Milli had been waiting for, but it meant questions being asked about the bruising on her eye. She decided honesty was the best policy.

On the day of the hospital trip, Milli dressed in the uniform she had been provided with: Black trousers along with closed-toed black shoes and a light pink tunic with black trim. Her ID and access badge had arrived a few days before with a picture, ID number and name on it. She had followed the instructions to scan her retina onto the back surface allowing her to activate the ID. Often thumb prints were required for an ID card, but on this one they had taken eye details instead. She felt ready and was quietly pleased her father had organised a private transport to take her to the hospital. On arrival at the reception desk she found others from her course stood or sat waiting. She smiled, waved and wandered over. The lady in the group she was closest to, Dawn, winced and looked at her face.

'How did you do that?!' Milli frowned and shook her head.

'I have no idea, but I have had it checked out and it doesn't hurt me at all. We have been using poultices to draw out the bruise, but I think I need to stop using them as it's affecting the white of my eye…' Dawn agreed.

'I would, that looks funny! Maybe someone here needs to look at it?' Again, Milli shook her head.

'No, no need, I feel fine…' She would have gone on but the professionals from the hospital had arrived and so her first shift began.

She was pleased to be teamed with Dawn, and the pair had gone from patient to patient checking bloods and vital signs, supporting people to get comfortable and helping with anything the professionals asked. As they walked down a small corridor heading towards the CT scan area,

Milli got the strangest feelings in her gut. She stopped and looked about her. Something wasn't right: she felt so anxious and upset. She looked about the corridor but could not see anything that would make her worried; she certainly didn't feel anyone was following her. This was different; the anxious feeling was in her core, right down to the bone, to her very soul. As Milli was trying to get her head around her sudden anxiety, a porter, with doctor in attendance, had begun to walk towards them. On the glide-tech bed they were manoeuvring was a young man who had just come from the CT scanner. The boy looked pale, skin pulled taught with pain, making his features look almost skeletal. Milli froze as the three went past her and caught the words stating that there was nothing they could do.

Surprising Dawn with the suddenness of her movement, Milli spun on her heels and ran to catch up with the doctor and porter. Without even thinking she blurted out the question asking what was wrong with the boy. She had no idea what drove her, she knew she was talking out of turn, but could not stop herself; she felt driven to find out what was wrong. The doctor looked angry, but seeing her ID badge, changed his demeanour to come over as the higher professional giving some advice.

'I won't take insult that you have just stopped me for this, but be advised I don't take kindly to being demanded of an answer. This young man, regrettably, has had an accident causing grave damage to his nervous system.' That was all she needed to know, and she bobbed her head and returned to Dawn.

'He is going to be on our ward later.' She would see him later.

Zyman had been resting in his own room, taking time to fill out his diary, have some food and bathe. The time he had been covering for Oroch and Makkan had taken it out of him a little, but he was now feeling much better. On returning from the bathroom, he was getting dressed when he stopped, looking closely in the mirror before him. His hand raised slowly to touch the back of his shoulder. He suddenly turned his head trying to see over his shoulder to his shoulder blade, but he couldn't. A shimmer of green had caught his eye as he was getting dressed and his searching hand had found scales on his shoulder that shimmered the same as those around his eye. Did this happen to the older generation; was it something missed from the history books? Lindany had said something about changes to Oroch. Pulling his shirt up over his shoulder and continuing to dress, his thoughts roamed through who he might need to speak to, and the leader of the old Walkers, Steve, was the only person he could think of.

'Lindany' he said out loud, leaving his room to find the Portal Walker.

Milli had found her time in the CT scanning area of the hospital fascinating, but each patient that had come in with some suspected injuries of some kind or other all seemed to be clear. The group had discussed whether this was a waste of resources, but all agreed better to be safe than sorry. Someone came up with the idea of finding a way to add such scanners to the medical robotic kits that you could call upon in your own home. Once the group were given leave to head back to their appointed ward stations,

Milli and Dawn had left, talking amicably. Just before they reached the entrance to their ward, Dr Bannerman stepped in their way, blocking entry. She looked at the pair for a long moment before speaking in the softest of tones.

'Dawn, Milli, a young gentleman has come onto the ward with damage to the nerve endings in the base of his spine. He will not gain use of his legs again as no medication in the holds can cure such injuries. His family are with him, but I wanted to speak with you first. The family and the young man know the score and are happy for you to support and help to provide what care is required, and to look at the statistics on his monitors, but are you ready for this level of care? This is your first practical shift, so I need to know that you can emotionally handle this.' Her tone was supportive, but Milli couldn't help but note how the doctor held eye contact with Milli as she spoke. Both students agreed that they were ready, agreeing that they would seek support if not. Milli fidgeted with her uniform as she was introduced to the family, but as soon as she looked at the skeletal features of the boy, her emotions became such a turmoil she was not sure what came over her. She stepped forward and began looking at the boy, her hands going to move the monitors out of the way so she could get closer to his body. Her mind had shut out all the ward around her, as she sought the cause of the young boy's paralysis. Though the boy was lying on his back, his dignity covered with the bed sheets, as Milli's hands hovered above his hip line, it was as though she could see the breaks, as though her imagination was transposing the image to her mind's eye. Without stopping to consult anyone, she closed her eyes and drew upon her dragonic nature that she had no idea was there.

'What are you doing!!!!?' Called Dr Bannerman as she faced Milli on the opposite side of the bed. Dawn was about to wrap her arms around Milli to stop her, but the shocked cry from their tutor froze her in her place. Milli had looked up, saying

'I can do this.' She had met the doctor's eyes with her own mismatched ones. Where the bruising had been, green scales now rippled; the draconic eye with its iris closed to a slit held the doctors gaze, challenging her desire to make her stop. The doctor was physically shaking, but at this moment, Milli didn't register the fact. Looking back down, she closed her eyes, holding her arms out over the boy and focused. It was like roots that had been cut - like the delicate stem of a flower that had been trodden on or broken by the wind. The energy flowed through her like the most natural thing in the world. Her arms and hands responded to the amount of magic needed by slowly covering with scales, the claws on her elongated fingers spanning out to cover the area she was concentrating on. The air around her became still as everyone froze at the sight, her breath regulated as she concentrated on knitting the nerves back to health. It was as if this scene held for an age. Once Milli instinctively knew her job had been done, she let out a long breath and opened her eyes. That was the moment everything came into sharp focus, including the expressions on everyone's faces, her hands slowly returning to human form and the sheer panic that was rising in Milli overspilled.

In that split second when the panic hit, Milli recalled everything. She registered the slightest of touches of the Stone as she slipped to the floor at the parade; how she had caught a glimpse of the light rippling across the surface of the Stone, her headaches, the conversations with the dragon in her mind – it all came flooding back to her. Milli screamed and stepped away from everyone in the ward.

'Stay away…' She cried out as her mind reeled. Had she somehow stolen one of the souls? Was this the reason the dragon of the mist had unleashed his power on Warwick? What had she done? She stared at her now human hands, then looked up at the group around her. The boy was sitting up with eyes like saucers. The doctor and Dawn were staring at her with a mixture of confusion, shock and worry. Out the corner of her eye, Milli caught a glimpse of her reflection and saw the dragon's eye looking back at her, marking her as a DragonWalker.

'What am I going to do? What am I going to do?!' The panic rose to the point where she didn't register the reassurance that was thrumming through her from Yebby. She couldn't go back to the wilds - she had stolen from them. She could not stay here as she had disobeyed a doctor, used magic on a patient and what place did a DragonWalker have in the metallic holds anyway? She should go home, speak to her father: he would help her. No, she couldn't drag her family into this. No, she needed to get away - far away - and then try and figure out what she was going to do. She had not realised that this was irrational thinking caused by the shock of everything that had just happened. She looked at her friend with tears beginning to stream down her cheeks.

'Tell my family…' Tell them what? She loved them? She was sorry? Milli didn't finish the sentence before she ran - one hand covering her eye, the other fumbling to get her ID ready for any obstacles ahead, not looking at who she ran around, not seeing who she bumped into but running as fast as she could to get out of the hospital. On a couple of occasions, by pushing a door or bouncing off a porter or fellow nurse, her hand would slip away from her eye, and each time her mind registered the gasp of shock at seeing her face; but she just kept running.

Once on the streets of Coventry she began to calm slightly. Using her chipped wrist, she bought some glasses which had the reflective surface that had come back into fashion recently. She had thought about a hat of some kind but felt that would make her stand out more as most individuals in the holds did not wear hats with their suits. With her eye covered she began to walk slower, her heartbeat and breathing calming, and slowly she merged in with all the other people in the streets, not looking at strangers.

'There she is!!!!' Eric shouted as he suddenly ripped the VR headset off his head, with enough force to send it flying across the room. Milan had almost choked on his drink as Eric had made him jump.

'Who?'

'I have found her! Yebby has finally used her power and I have her now. Reports in of a DragonWalker using magic in the main student hospital here in Coventry. She healed a young boy who is now crying miracle that he can walk again, and people throughout the hospital are shouting about a girl fleeing the scene with the markings of the Walker.... Why has she run?' Milan was wide eyed at the news and slowly began to rise from his chair. 'We need to go now.' Eric spoke with the authority of a leader. Milan went to point out that they should let Zyman know, and the

Governors of the hold, but the expression on Eric's face made him bite his tongue, and he opened a portal in front of the hospital.

From their sudden arrival onwards, Milan was not hiding his markings, and nobody questioned why they were there. The young Royal and the Walker were shown directly to where Dawn, Dr Bannerman, the young boy and his family still sat in quiet shock. Milan held up his hand as he entered and smiled.

'Please, we are here to talk…' and with that they began to ask as many questions as required to gain information on what might have happened.

Zyman didn't need anyone to tell him something had just happened. He had been making his way out into the market, where he had been informed that Lindany had gone to the inn, when he stumbled forward onto one knee. For a moment, he felt drained of all energy. Breathing heavily, he held his hand to his chest to gain his composure. As he calmed, and the feeling of balance returned, he carried on his journey, but rather than heading towards his original goal, he continued walking, making his way to the woodland in the distance. He left the path as soon as he could and found a quite space next to a large oak to rest against. He closed his eyes and drew in a deep breath, going into his mind to ask his dragon for advice on what he had just felt.

# Chapter 11

# The Hunted

Still sitting beside the old tree, Zyman opened his eyes to look directly at a young boy standing in front of him. It took the Walker a moment to register that the boy seemed to be waiting for him. Zyman stretched his back, then stood, frowning, focused on the young boy. The boy wore the colours of Warwick's Royal crest. His hair was damp, his cheeks flushed, and he seemed to be fidgeting with energy and impatience, although he was trying to be respectful of Zyman. Taking a deep breath, Zyman smiled.

'You have a message for me?' The boy nodded far too quickly and almost seemed to hop as he blurted out the message that Zyman was needed in the holding chamber. The Walker placed his hands on his hips and nodded that he understood the message. Before he had said thanks, the boy was gone - more errands to complete for his wage today. Zyman bowed his head for a moment, trying to gather his thoughts before heading back to the castle. His DragonSoul did not seem to have answers on all the subjects that were bothering the Natural Walker, but he had been encouraging and kept repeating that all was ok. He rolled his eyes and barked a strange sounding chuckle to himself.

'We'll see…eighteen years of age and already so sceptical!' he said out loud before raising his head and walking back to the castle. As he walked through the streets of Warwick, his eyes caught sight of different people who brought back memories of simpler times; most smiled back if they saw him.

Entering the Castle, Zyman took a moment to adjust to the cooler light reflecting from the thick grey stone of his home. The atmosphere was light, with people going about their business. His eyes caught Tellany in the distance, and he changed his direction to catch up with the Earth Walker for a moment. They exchanged news on how things were going, bantering and chuckling about the evening's antics he heard about and the news from the council chamber. As the reports were 'all's well', Zyman clapped his fellow Walker on the shoulder in thanks and carried on his way. After a time, he reached the room that he secretly felt made the split between metallic holds and the wilds the myth it was. If someone was tagged and chipped to come to the wilds, this room held the data. If medicines, supplies, fuels, electric anything from the holds was required, it was dealt with in this room. If the Governors of any hold wished to talk with the wilds, it was done from this room. This room was the data centre of the wilds and the link which had been keeping all informed of the damages, taking requests for help. Emails, calls, news feeds, media influence, weather charts - it was all here; in fact, it was how they knew that the balance of the elements was working across the land. If Glasgow started having fluctuating unnatural weather, the data was here. Gaining his composure, Zyman entered the holding chamber, without knocking. The sight that met him always grated slightly. Half of the room was taken up with a glass surface that was concave: a semicircle screen shimmering with a slightly neon blue hue. To one side was a hub of wires, routers, servers and several banks of computers; the hum of equipment permanently in the background was guaranteed to raise his irritation level. A small screen was placed next to the servers as a visual aid in monitoring their condition. A small gentleman wearing a suit was sitting in the same corner as the monitor, his eyes flicking from systems to monitors as he endeavoured to keep the hub of technology working. Zyman wandered over to him and stood looking at the shimmering glass and asked:

'What's up?' The technician smiled and indicated he should stand directly in front of the screen.

'A call is being held from Eric.' Zyman simply raised one eyebrow but moved as requested and waited for the screen to come to life. This screen was the closest the wilds got to Virtual Reality. It enabled someone from a metallic hold who was accessing the virtual space to commune with someone in this room. To the person in VR, Zyman would look like he was talking on a flat square screen, as had been the case when Skype was utilised back in the early 2000s. But Zyman would see the avatar of the person in the VR space.

'Ok, load the call.'

The arc of glass slowly changed, and then before him was a room devoid of all furnishings apart from a chair and table, an Exit door and a fake window that showed an evening setting of Coventry. Sitting in the chair was his twin brother, looking nothing like he was used to. This Eric, his hair still spiked as usual, was wearing a grey three-piece suit, the white of his collar sharp against the dusk grey colour of the jacket and waistcoat. The jacket was cut long in length and flared out where it lay against the chair, Eric having only the top three buttons done up. His legs were crossed, but the fit of the almost black trousers with the seam down the front, the boot leg hems stopping at shining black shoes gave a very striking image. Zyman had to admit that he suited the look, but it still disturbed him.

'Eric, why the call? You have Milan with you; come home and let us discuss in the flesh.'

'No can do brother, I am too busy to leave here. You know the pace of these holds and, if I miss but a moment, I could lose her.'

'What is going on Eric?' His tone was slightly exasperated, which he regretted, but this room always got to him. Eric heard the tone and caught Zyman off guard by answering in a slightly condescending tone.

'Don't you know?' he paused for a moment, then, smiling in a way that sent a slight-chill up the Walker's back, his brother explained: 'We found her. Yebby has manifested in a young holder girl called Milli. While on shift at the hospital, this girl worked a miracle of manipulating nerves back to health, but then ran. Witnesses believe she did not know what she was doing, or she was acting on instinct.' Eric rose from his chair then, his suit jacket falling to wrap around his thighs to just above his knees. 'I had been searching media day and night and stumbled across a news feed from the day of the parade. This girl, when falling, touched the DragonSoul Stone, and we believe must have seen the Stone. Her tutor has confirmed she spoke of seeing a dragon in her dreams.' He shook his head then and for a moment looked remorseful. 'I missed it. I saw the clip but dismissed it because, from the angle showed on the news feed, it looked like she fell beside the float. I thought nothing of it; I was stupid.' He looked back at Zyman, emanating a growing anger as he paced the virtual room. 'It was across the news feed then, the incident in the hospital. Milan took me straight to the site, and we questioned some of the witnesses who all confirmed the condition of her eyes.' Zyman pulled his thoughts back to the conversation, away from the mind-blowing information he had just learnt about his powers and winced as he knew what would be coming up next as Eric continued. 'You're going to have the Governors breathing down your neck and for that I am sorry, but speed was of the essence. We lost her for a time but gained access to her parents. We spoke to them both and they explained how she had been since the parade. Foolish girl thought she was having nightmares of a dragon in her dreams. Following advice from her lecturer, she tried to calm her mind and work out what her anxieties were, not realising that what she was doing was beginning to talk to the DragonSoul. I realise she did not know what she was doing, but if that was the case why has she run? That soul is mine!' Zyman was not sure if his brother meant to say that last statement out loud, but it was a whispered line that worried him. He continued as if the last statement had not shaken him:

'Where is she now, Eric?'

'While I was with her family, they got a message via LMS apologising for what she was about to do. By all accounts she then accessed her family's driving account and has entered the superslab in one of her father's cars.' In the space around Eric, a new window opened, and he swiped it to turn it around to show Zyman. The Walker stepped back at this and looked accusingly at his brother.

'you have retinal data now?' but Eric didn't take any notice and continued on.

‘We can see that the car is programmed to go to the Exeter wild. Why, we do not know, but we think that is the only other place she knows as it turns out her mother has some links down there. Distant links, but it was enough to put the name into her mind when she was running. I’m going to go after her.’

‘No Eric, come back here and we can send some of the Walkers. It might help her if she is talking to one of her own.’

‘Since when have I not been part of this?... I see, so the truth is there. I am not part of this at all am I? not since I stayed human?’

‘That is not what I meant; you *are* part of this, and we are trying to work things out. I just meant if she was to see another Walker, it might help her with any fears. We don’t want her power to turn to the negative. You understand that the Natural Walkers’ power of growth and harvest can turn to decay, pestilence, withering…?’

‘And what, you think I can’t handle the situation? That I would want to hurt the soul she has? Give me more credit *John!!*’

The twin brothers stared at each other for a moment, their eyes boring into each other as if trying to push their will on the other. Suddenly, Eric shrugged his shoulders, went back to his chair and sat down, almost nonchalantly leaning onto the table.

'Whatever you say. Do what you think is best. This is taking more out of you than me.' He waved his hand once and his avatar disappeared, the glass reverting to shimmering with the neon blue hue of lifelessness.

A couple of things had really bothered Zyman - not least, what his brother meant by it affecting him more. His thoughts were his own as he nodded to the technician and left the room. Not human… is that what this is about? He really had no idea what his brother was going to do, but he needed to put some plans into action fast.

Milli slept. She fell into a deep sleep as soon as she was on her way out of Coventry. She had secured the car using her family credentials. Milli hoped that her father understood the situation, with the message from her and the news filters he was bound to see, so he would not stop the vehicle remotely. She had clamped down all the locks, dimmed the windows and drifted off while the auto-drive glided her along the superslab towards Exeter. Just before falling asleep, her mind had drifted to a memory from her early years when she had taken her father's car because she wanted to go and see the sheep migration, as the farmers brought the flocks across the fields, which she had been told was a sight to behold. She remembered stamping her feet in frustration when she looked out the window and realised they were not moving, and she was still in the garage.

Eric removed the Virtual Reality headset with a sigh and looked over to Milan.

'Why do I always end up snapping at him! John is right, they have more chance of bringing Milli in; but he does rub it in my face - so unthoughtful at times. Not a consideration as to how I might be feeling, nor thanks for all the work I have done! Anyway, the main thing is, that once the girl is back in Warwick, she can let the soul go and all will be as it should be!' He paused to sigh, resigned to being the one thing he hated the most - patient. ‘I have done my bit. I set out to find her and I have.’ He threw the headset on to the bed behind him and was beginning to remove the straps when a knock at the door stopped all motion in the room. For a split second he thought about leaving the room. Instead he stood up, straightened his trousers, from where the straps had been, and began to remove the straps from his arms.

‘Milan, go to Zyman and report to him all that has happened. That might help smooth things over with him, don't you think?’ The Walker nodded in agreement. Eric wouldn’t admit it, but Zyman’s look had worried him. They had always been close, and part of Eric missed his brother. Shaking off his thoughts, Eric walked towards the door. Just as Eric began to open the door, the shimmer of light in the room showed a portal was just closing.

Eric opened the door, intending to ask the individual why they felt the need to disturb him, but words failed him as his eyes met those of the lady before him. Appearing to be in her late 30s, the lady stood in front of him matching his height, with striking hair that was blond, short and spikey, with the tips frosted grey. The colour of the tips matched her very pale complexion, which seemed to enhance her strong brown eyes, accented with eye liner and thick mascara. Piercing her earlobes were large golden hoop earrings, large enough to practically reach the shoulder pads which she had in her suit. She had a curvaceous figure, accentuated in all the right places, but was only just holding her in place. Her legs tapered down to thin ankles which supported pointed heeled shoes that looked uncomfortable to wear. In front of her was a small clutch bag, held in hands that dripped with bracelets and slender fingers adorned with rings and finely manicured silver nails. She didn't say a word; she simply looked at Eric's face and very slowly looked him down and back up. The corner of her lip turned up, showing the edge of pristine white teeth, before she put her hand on the door, moving it so she could enter. She did not ask for permission and, as she wandered into the room, Eric followed her with his gaze and for once was lost for words. Finally finding his voice, Eric asked what in faith she was doing and would she mind explaining herself. For quite some time she said nothing just wandered round his room taking in the magazine choice from where Milan had been sitting, the VR headset on the bed, the disarray in the bathroom doorway yet to be cleaned up. On finishing her inspection, she turned quickly round, smiled broadly and held out both arms as if to embrace Eric; Eric didn't move.

'Eric. Coventry has been good to you. You look refreshed, for which I am glad. Seeing you after the ceremony, when you rushed from the hall, I was most distraught for you. I felt your pain.' She raised an eyebrow and, placing a hand on her squeezed-together chest, she feigned being upset. 'I can tell by your face you didn't see me there. You don't recognise me at all, but I have known you for many years. Ahh yes, You and John used to insist on trying to attend meetings with your father.' She hummed to herself as she wandered over to sit in the seat Milan had vacated. She absently began to finger the corner of the magazine, slapping her hand down on the cover once she realised, she was doing it. 'I'm hurt Eric. How could you forget me?? Ahh well, my fault for not remembering your birthdays or holidays this year... or any year for that matter... but I digress; I shall introduce myself anew. My name is Prudence. Governess Prudence to be more specific. I am one of the Governors of Coventry, who should be highly irritated right now that you did not inform them of your presence in the hold, Oh, I *am* irritated, but not as much as others so you are lucky!' the accented wording of 'oh I am' made Eric cringe slightly, but he had finally gained his composure and went to sit down at the table, on the opposite chair. The table was to the side of the room, so he leaned his back against the wall, his arm hooked over the back of the chair as he slowly crossed his legs.

'Governess Prudence, I am sorry I did not recognise you - much has happened.'

'Yes, Yes, terrible, all of it, but enough with the pleasantries; how are you doing getting your soul?' Prudence slowly turned to face Eric, with her expression moulded into a polite smile. She didn't wait for him to answer. 'I smoothed over all that business with the Governors here, so you needn't worry about that my dear, though I am surprised your brother didn't get in touch once he realised what had happened. Left it for you to deal with I see?' She slowly shook her head, clicking her tongue lightly as if disappointed that this should have happened to Eric. 'He must be far too busy to help his brother when he really needs it, but that's ok because it has drawn out, shall we say, 'qualities' in you. Knew where to look for information - clever.'

Eric hadn't been thinking along those lines about John, and it made him frown.

'Don't scowl, your face is far too beautiful for that; besides, what's done is done. Your brother is going to take immediate action now, isn't he? John doesn't want that girl to get used to having the soul. My apologies, Zyman does realise that, right? That the longer this goes on, the stronger the bond?' Prudence drew out this last sentence, letting it settle before nodding. 'I am sure Zyman has it all in hand and will do what is best for you, as he has done up until now. But, right now, I must go.' Rising from her chair, her skirt only just managing to contain her, she took one last look about the room before striding out. As she pulled the door behind her, Eric heard Governess Prudence say 'Welcome to Coventry, Royal Eric' and the door slammed shut.

Milan found Eric still sitting in the same place at the table when he returned from his meeting with Zyman. Eric smiled at his friend, but it was a look that wasn't reflected in his eyes. He asked how the meeting had gone.

'Zyman is going to ask some of the Walkers to accompany him to Exeter, where the girl is going, but wants her to find her place in the surroundings so they can talk to her without scaring her off. He said, and I quote, 'best to take our time and for her to work with us rather than rush and prolong her running'. Something odd passed across Eric's features as he replied simply with

'Really'.

# Chapter 12

# Pieces of the Puzzle

The ageing ex-Walker Steve was sitting quietly in a local ale house. He had almost reached his destination and was enjoying taking his time looking about Dorset. As he remembered it, Dorset had said 'no' to the dragons' offer and, with no Royals among the DragonWalkers, had slowly fallen by the wayside within the dynamics of the wilds. The people were pleasant, the sights and sounds like other wilds he had visited, the atmosphere calm yet, as his eyes scanned the landscape, he got the feeling that the metallic holds that blocked out its horizons had turned their back on this place. To someone used to the ways of Warwick, it felt like there was no energy in the surroundings. Over the period of the journey, Steve's guards and guide riders had been let go one by one. Finally, it was just himself and one guide. The bond between the two, ex-Walker and Guide, had deepened and grown into a friendship. The pair now sat amicably at a fine oak bar, their backs to the room, hands cupped around mugs of ale and talking about anything that entered their minds. For an old stone building it was surprisingly well lit, enabling you to watch shadows of whoever passed it dance on the walls. The staff were polite, the air fresh and the whole place gave off a scent of cleanliness.

'You would expect the ale to be flat in a sterile place like this, but its actually pretty good!' Steve agreed with his colleague, raising his mug and taking a deep drink.

'Not long now, Steve, until we are back in Exeter - even if we have taken a roundabout way of getting there! First you turn down a portal; I understand why. Then, we go a route no guide would suggest! But, I am *not* complaining.'

After pausing to take a drink, he continued 'So, once we reach Exeter, what are you going to do then Steve?'
Steve looked to his friend and shrugged.

'No idea. Some reading I think; taking time and don't forget the basket weave...' The door to the inn opened, and voices halted the friendly conversation.

'Did you hear?! They have a rogue Walker! I know, healed a boy in Coventry then ran. That Royaling Eric is on the lookout for her, but for some reason the Walkers are sitting tight!' said a rather nasally voice.

'I heard they are angry with her for stealing the soul.'

'I heard that the Governess of Coventry is on the rampage because if she was joined in Coventry then she should belong to them...'

'I heard that she has gone into hiding, making a den out of vines, and looking super creepy. Half dragon, half human.'

'Fools!' Steve sighed before he could stop himself. He turned to the group of people who had entered and were talking about the recent events. He was off his chair and walking towards the group before his friend could cough out his ale and splutter

‘STOP’. Steve managed to get his composure just before he reached the group. Taking a deep breath, he straightened his shoulders as much as he could and cleared his throat.

‘Excuse me. I couldn't help but over-hear. Would you mind telling me where this information came from? When you heard it?’ For a moment there was complete silence, each person looking to the next before back to Steve, who was looking a little suspicious, what with his ageing years yet strong voice and his eye patch. Finally, the nasally speaker who had started the conversation nodded.

‘We travel between the wilds laying hedgerows and doing stone work. Call us rural craftsmen if you will. None of us made it to the Parade, but that don't stop a man from having an interest.’ All the group nodded, and he continued. ‘We have come up from Exeter, and the air was a buzz with the Walkers who had saved the quay. Sucked the water right out to sea, they did - it was some impressive work. We were asked by the Royal family there to help with the damaged shop fronts, which we did. nice job too...’ The conversation paused as three ale mugs were placed in front of the group. Steve and his guide retrieved their own ale mugs and sat down with the group.

'This story sounded like dry work. Please...' He indicated the drinks and waited for the conversation to start flowing again. Some story it appeared to be too, humans turning into lizards, tornados into portals, healed nervous systems, and a Walker on the run. Steve was sitting quietly as he was trying to take it all in. His mind was reeling. Finally, the nasally voice ran out of steam enabling another person to take up the story. His voice was deep and brooding as he spoke clear and slow.

'I ain't from Exeter way, but I heard that Royal Eric has been in talks with the Governors. It was on all the displays as we came through Bristol to meet these guys here' indicating that they hadn't travelled together. 'Pictures of them on the feeds shaking hands, pictures of them in discussions, he is quite the looker when he is suited and booted.' All nodded as if they had all seen this news. As the arrival of the ale had created camaraderie around the table, so finishing the drinks drew the conversation to a close. Steve and his friend rose and thanked them. He did not return to the bar but, with a look and stance that made him appear much older than he was, he shuffled out of the bar, his friend following. He needed to find out more information. The governess's interactions had stirred a memory that was plucking at his aging mind but fading too soon to grasp. Why was Coventry suddenly so interested in Eric?

Text messages had been coming and going between Governess Prudence and Eric with growing intensity. At first, he had shown each one to Milan with comments of 'what is she saying?' and 'like I would want to go to the meeting', but the Purple Walker had noticed that this was no longer the case. Instead, Eric focused on his device and had the nervous twitch of someone constantly checking their phone. Considering he had only had the phone since being in Coventry, this was what was unnerving Milan the most. The two were spending an evening at a restaurant, which Prudence had recommended, and yes, the food had been amazing, but Milan had felt truly out of place for the first time. Eric felt comfortable watching the people walk by and the scrolling scenery on the window display screens. He was at ease choosing the menu from the holographic boards in the centre of the table, but Milan had felt anxious. It took him a while to realise that it was his DragonSoul radiating this emotion, and he couldn't get away from the feeling that this was all wrong. He was dressed in a white shirt with its top button undone and purple trousers. Eric was in his three-piece suit, which was fast becoming his chosen style of dress. Milan blinked and looked down at the cuffs of his shirt.

'We could have eaten in our room.' Eric didn't respond but looked over to his friend and shrugged.

'it makes a change of air to be out.' Eric looked back down to the displays shimmering on the glass table, his hand lazily changing the social stream to find one that interested him while Milan continued to fidget with his cuffs, then his collar. His eyes scanned the room and he couldn't help but notice the few people who gawked at his face before whispering. For a moment he raised his hand to cover the dragon eye, his fingers almost touching his face when he suddenly changed his mind and instead used it to push his chair away from the table.

'Change of air, good idea. I'm going outside for a moment.' He headed outside and stood in the doorway unsure of which way to walk. Out of the corner of his eye, he spotted a small shop which had its displays covered by what looked like vine, the name on the sign being Covenstree. He was drawn to the green like a moth to flame and headed down to hover outside the shop. Milan stood looking at the variety of plants for sale for a moment. The owner came out to ask if there was something he wanted, a tablet computer in hand to take his order but, on being declined a sale he soon left Milan to his thoughts. Milan stood there for – he wasn't sure how long - but feeling once more in control, he headed back. He took the mobile he had been given out of his pocket. For a moment he stopped and stared at its black inactive surface before shoving it back into his pocket and walking back to the restaurant with more purpose in his stride. As Milan made his way back to the table, he was not surprised to see Prudence sitting in his seat. She raised a hand in greeting before pretty much dismissing his presence and finishing what she was saying.

'Yes, that's right, we believe that having you on the Board would promote a positive ethos between wilds and holds.' Prudence glanced out of the window before turning back to Eric, 'You should consider it as an honour. Besides, your being part of Coventry has more chance of happening than you getting your soul.'

Eric almost hissed when Milan took a step closer to the table.

'What? Did I hit a nerve? I do apologise, but you have to admit that all chances of getting that soul are slipping away. How are you going to get it? You do understand that the DragonSoul Stone is no longer active? You are the only other living person who has touched the stone. So, you kill the girl and the soul has nowhere else to go.' Milan and Eric froze, looking at Prudence with eyes wide and faces losing all colour. Prudence took a sip from the glass in front of her, seemingly oblivious to the fact that it wasn't hers. She swallowed, winced and looked over to Milan waving the bottom of the glass towards him.

‘No alcohol? Wonder what a Walker would look like with a little wine in them hmmm?’ Milan took offence at the remark and straightened his back. Taking a leaf out of Eric’s book, he tugged on his sleeve cuffs to straighten them.

‘Wine dulls the senses and slows the mind.’ He finished the line looking directly at the Governess. As she placed the glass down and began to rise, she spoke to Milan in a very different tone.

‘It would pay you to show just a little more respect, half-breed.’ Spinning round, she then said good night to Eric as if everything had been absolutely peachy and went on her way. Milan slipped back into his seat.

‘Did you hear her? Half-breed!! Did you... Oi, Eric!!’ That snapped the Royal back to focus on the room. Eric seemed to shake it off, ran his fingers through his hair and then placed his hands on his cutlery. Absently straightening the fork next to the knife, he spoke to the nearest waiter.

‘Our food is taking too long!’

Shuffling and bowing, the waiter disappeared, and Eric turned back to Milan. ‘Kill the girl or work as a governor. Interesting choices. Prudence does have a way of explaining things. We were discussing politics before you arrived. She was asking my opinion and is going to action some of my suggestions.’

‘What? Eric, they’re not your only choices. By the balance, there is more out there than just that.’ Milan was lost for words, his own mind stumbling over the realisation that he was a half-breed and, for the first time, airing a suggestion on how to solve the issue. ‘Why don’t we go back and talk to Zyman?’ …and that was the wrong thing to say. Eric smacked his hand on the cutlery and rose from the table.

‘I will not go running off to my brother at the first major snag we have come across. For status in this world, I, above everyone, now have two options open to me. You go back if you want to, but Me? I’m going to take in the sights of the night life of Coventry.’

Milan went to follow him, but he wasn’t fast enough as Eric was on the streets and gone.

Milli had stayed in the car for as long as she could. It had been a cold night, and she had been glad that her father had not recalled the vehicle. She was pretty sure it would get recalled eventually, but for now she was glad of its shelter, the whirring heater being the only noise in her metallic cocoon. She had spent some time staring at her hands, noting their fully human form but her memory overlaying draconic claws and green scales. She had replayed the hospital incident over and over in her mind, but strangely, her emotions had shifted with each repeat. Fear, shock and horror had been her initial feelings, but they were now overtaken by wonder, awe and excitement. She was a DragonWalker!! Her soul had confirmed that as she had done her version of meditation along the superslab. Her DragonSoul was named Yebby, and she was now a Natural Walker. Milli had not received the teachings to know she should take on the dragon's name as an honorific, nor that the pair should only commune when meditating. The two were becoming one within her body, but their minds stayed their own. Milli, someone from a metallic hold, someone who was not Royal, special or anything else, was a DragonWalker. Communing with her dragon soul had helped her in understanding the magic she now held: growth, healing and the natural world were her positive magic, but she got the feeling the opposite would be true for the negative. She did not really want to think about that. The dragon explained the balance, the other elements, and other powers within. Once her mind had accepted this fact, her thoughts had turned to the future and what the hell she was going to do! She needed food, shelter, a job; she also needed to charge her phone! How was she going to access Virtual Reality?!! Her dragon had tried to point out that she could go to Warwick, but the flash of sheer terror that had caused put a stop to such thoughts. No, they wouldn't appreciate her turning up now. Much time had passed, and they had got into their roles; Zyman was the leader and that was settled. No, she had touched the Stone and looked upon the Dragonstone which was forbidden; there would not be a place for her there.

Finally, as the sun came up, Milli reluctantly left the vehicle and wandered away from the tarmac of the superslab and stepped onto the tracks of the wilds. It never crossed her mind that she could have been picked up through the night by a lockdown instigated by the authorities. As she moved further away from the car, she became curious of her surroundings and felt more at home. - any chance of understanding the position she had been in through the night slipping away with each passing step. As the tracks wound their way towards Exeter, Milli's eyes scanned the horizon, wandered over the fields, her senses taking in the sights and sounds around her. She felt that she was seeing things with a little more clarity than her visit to Warwick: the green a little more vibrant; the blue more like her beloved MMORPG Morla; and the sounds now included the occasional buzzing of a passing bee, the motion of a vole on the bank or the distant bark of a farm dog possibly running to its master. It was all very intoxicating; Milli found herself enjoying the walk with Yebby, and both began to relax.

As Milli approached the edges of the Exeter Wild she realised that she had to be practical. She needed a roof over her head, food in her belly and, if possible, some way of getting a fresh start. She was still wearing her 'metallic-styled' clothes and her reflective sunglasses, which she had got on leaving the hospital; all looked a little worse for wear. She wandered slowly towards the centre of Exeter, guided by the sound of water and walked in the direction of the quay. She walked past the cathedral, past the array of shops and headed towards the place where, not so long ago, Oroch, Makkan and Lindany had helped with the storm damage. Standing on the very bridge they had used to work their magic, Milli took some deep breaths then looked for the nearest tailor. On spotting the very shop she was looking for, she made a decision and acted upon it. Smiling politely at the lady serving her, she looked at some of the work and found an outfit to her liking: a simple skirt, white short sleeved top, cuffs that matched the colour of the skirt to wrap around her wrists and a beautifully crafted belt. Confirming that holder credits were accepted, she brought the clothing and left the shop.

In the next shop, Milli purchased some leather-worked footwear and a small pouch for holding her few valuables. The conversation in both shops had been polite with nothing seeming amiss. Requesting permission to change her clothes on the premises, Milli left the area feeling more confident and comfortable with the surroundings. After purchasing food items, a few cooking implements and a small mug, she headed away from Exeter's centre towards the forest, not realising she was being drawn to the area previously prepared by the group of diplomats. Perhaps the echo of their magic still lingered there, but Milli was pleasantly surprised to find the marked-out area, the fire pit and the foliage, giving her good cover and a view. Sitting on the very log that Makkan had sat on, the severity of her situation slowly became clearer. Was this how she was now going to live? Could she survive? She took her phone out of her pocket for a moment and looked at its black inactive screen. Her thumb hovered over the screen ready to swipe it into life but, without finishing the motion, she put her phone back into her pouch as silent tears slowly started to run down her cheeks. All the emotions she had been through in the last however many hours crashed around her until she was sobbing into her hands. Light in the area faded, day turning to dusk as she slowly brought herself around from her reverie. This was not helping anyone, and she needed to take some action. Dusk turned to night as Milli gained her composure. Her mind began to focus on what she understood of the Natural Walkers - of what she was - and remembered her readings. 'So, though I have the full power of nature, I have limited skill in all four elements.' Slowly she stood and looked toward the vegetation that was in front of her. Closing her eyes and raising her hand she began to imagine the upturned tree roots extending in an arc up and around her, the shrubbery thickening, the vines tangling all they touched until an open-sided dome surrounded the area. Her ears caught the sound of shuffling, and she knew that her image was becoming a reality - the land responding to her bidding. She continued to work but opened her eyes to witness the glistening scales of her hands, the miracle of growth that was happening around her. Her imagination began to take hold as flowers slowly lined the base of the construction and roots began to protrude from the side of the dome, inwards towards her, to create seating and a small table, and moss blossoming to create an area for a bed. As her imagination developed and the image formed, her magic pulsed within her. Unnoticed, the scales had spread down her side. She continued working until the area was unrecognisable. As the final leaf fell, it completed the cover that camouflaged the dome. Milli turned to the fire and with a flick of her hand, flames burst from the wood. The flames coming to life so suddenly and so easily made her jump, and she came back to reality with a bump. Eyes wide with amazement, she looked at her achievement and smiled. Now she knew she had a home. She tried summoning water but with no luck, so she left the safety of her home to go and find a natural spring. It didn't take her long to find the natural source of life as many animal tracks led to the same area. Returning to the safety of her tree-dome, she cooked a simple soup and spent the rest of her waking hours staring at the view in front of her. The slight shimmer of the distant holds plucked at her emotions, but not as strongly now as her mind was slowly coming to terms with this new way of life.

Zyman had called all the Walkers together and was explaining what he knew of the rogue DragonSoul. All were showing a mixed array of emotions. One day Zyman would wonder if the emotions matched the elements but, for now, he was not surprised that Fire Walker Ethany (formerly known as Chris) was suggesting quick action or that Earth Walker Tellany was suggesting a steady plan of action. Each suggestion that was being thrown at Zyman, he felt as though he had thought of already and dismissed; - he needed something new.

'I'm telling you, we should just go pick her up and explain all to her once she is here. If she was so excited to come to the procession, then she will have enough respect for us to comply.'

'That won't work, we need to let her settle in wherever she is and let her learn her soul before we go charging in. We don't know what damage it might cause at this tender state.'

‘Look, I am telling you just go and get her…’

‘No. We need to consider what we are going to do with her once we have her here…’ The voice that spoke stopped the whole room and everyone turned to look at Milan, who had just entered the room looking tired, drawn and concerned. ‘What are we going to do? Welcome her into our council with no knowledge of the balance, of the ways of the wilds? Keep her prisoner until we find out how to give the soul to Eric? Demand she tell us how this happened in the first place?’ With each comment his eyes scanned the room, his draconic purple iris seeming to bore into each Walker sitting round the table. ‘This is not as simple as just going to collect the girl. You have forgotten that the soul was not meant for her, she has had no training. What if she turns her powers to the negative without thinking: could we stop that kind of outburst of power? Do we want to?’ He shrugged his shoulders and began to walk towards his seat. His fingers fidgeted with his cuffs, and sitting in the wild’s council with holder clothes on, he felt he stood out more than ever. ‘Eric is angry, he is hurting, and he is gaining support from others who are not us! You have left him to his own devices too long and ideas are being fed to him. I know this is not what this council was here to discuss, but I think the situations are intertwined, and you have all been ignoring the obvious.' Zyman was as still and silent as the others as Milan continued. 'She is metallic bred. The holders have a claim to her if they choose to execute that right. She has not filed with their systems for transfer, she has been an upstanding citizen until now and they are going to act how they choose. Holders running through the wilds looking for her? How will this look to the wilds they trample through?' His words were obviously shaking people as rain began to splatter on the windows. Zyman raised a hand to silence Milan. 'Oroch, Gilbran, calm your thoughts.' The two Water Walkers from Exeter took a moment, though the rain continued to fall. 'I have been in the holds for longer than I care to be, and they are a different breed to us. They stare, they whisper, they…' the recent incident in the restaurant in the back of his mind; but he cuts that thought process short and looks to Zyman. 'He is your brother and is a Royal. Eric needs our support now more than ever.' This final sentence made all around the table shuffle slightly and look at each other. Eventually Lindany looked to his brother Milan and asked where Eric was.

'I don't know. He ran out of the restaurant to sample the night life, and I have had no contact with him since. I returned to our hotel room hoping he would return. And this is the first time you ask?' Milan snapped the last sentence at Lindany before he finally sat down.

'I apologise brother, that was not meant as it sounded.'

The Purple Walker nodded and smiled. 'You have had quite a burden Simon, you don't have to apologise to me.' Using his original human name seemed to calm the brothers, and both nodded at each other before all eyes turned back to their leader. Zyman sighed and looked down to his hands, raising them up to look at his palms before clenching his fists.

'I am sorry to continue to ask this of you, but Gilbran, Ethany, Siska and Tellany, please continue to hold the balance from the council chamber. It is possibly going to get harder as the other Walkers do what they need to do, so

I need our strongest team on this. You four work best together with seamless understanding. Can I count on you?' All four nodded. Zyman continued. 'Oroch, Makkan & Lindany, I must request you to team up once more and go to Exeter in search of the Natural Walker. Do not force her into any direction currently. Talk to her; find out what her drive for running is; gain her trust.' As the three nodded, Zyman turned to Milan. 'I ask you to return to Coventry and support Eric, but I will go with you.' Zyman had shocked all with this statement but, before anyone could dwell on this, he had one final request to make. 'Fire Walker Musany and Earth Walker Bechany: it will be a long ride, but ride fast and find Steve. He is heading to Exeter but has stopped in Dorset at this time. This was the last known contact we had with the elder-Walker. He was the leader of this council for 50 years and, though he wishes to retire, we need his guidance. We need to know if he has any experience of the alterations that are marking all of us in this room. You have each had some experience of scales staying upon your skin, or other features being twisted slightly. I cannot help but feel this is something we are misunderstanding, something we need to investigate, but I can find no history of it in our books. Our souls hold the wisdom, and so far, none have resonated concern for us doing the wrong thing, but they are not speaking up. We need more help, and we need to try and find answers.' As the two final DragonWalkers nodded that they understood what they needed to do, it was also clear that nobody else had really thought about why the dragons were not speaking out about the growing changes and how to help with what could turn into a very negative situation. Zyman's final thought was, 'why did the Governess of Coventry stir such emotions in him when he knew nothing of her…?'

# Chapter 13

# Drawing Near

Coventry would never fall into darkness, the lights shimmering from the streets below lighting up the city from within while the stars glistened in the night sky. Prudence and her fellow Governors gathered within their rotunda room, all sat in silence as the governess spoke. Her tone was as clipped as her frosted hair, while the tapping of her nails beat out the seconds as they pass, her eyes going over each member in the room as she tells them the details of the last few hours. None challenged her and her tone was absolute.

‘Yes, brothers and sisters, I have seen the changes we were warned to be wary of. Time grows short and the magic is almost upon us. The young Royal Eric struggles to accept his loss, but the seed has been planted and, if he’s as determined as we hope then he could well strike at the Natural Walker, giving us all time to gain our power.’ Her tone became almost caustic as she bitterly added the latter points. ‘They have been draining the balance, or should I say the elements, for long enough. Their time will be with us again soon, and, unless our plans work, our own magic skills will wither as the dragons’ bodies did. They tell men that witches and warlocks held no power, and the humans did not question this. They tell humans that they will protect the balance with their wisdom, yet the humans fail to ask questions as to why!’ This last statement gained a few grumblings of agreement. ‘So much work and preparation, yet our plans to hold the Natural Walker almost lost due to the girl running away!’ At these last words, as if timed perfectly, the door to the chamber opened and three smartly-suited men walked in. The central one, held his head high, while the other two appeared to be pushing to make him enter more quickly. Milli's father held his head firm, and his eyes never wavered from Prudence.

'How many years planning, Tony? How many nights watching your young daughter grow into the perfect vessel for the soul. Everything in place, everything planned down to the wire.' She smirks as she adds, 'Slipping up at the last moment as you fail to bring your daughter back to Coventry. Explain'.

Tony's voice wavered as he responded.

'Lady Prudence, I beg your understanding. If I had returned the car that night, Milli would see me as not helping her. Milli would realise I was, that I was...'

'What? Not being a good father? Not being an understanding dad? I wonder...' Prudence rose from her chair and slowly walked round the table toward the trio of men standing at the side of the room. She stopped short and looked up at Milli's father. The imagery would have been funny if not for the electric atmosphere in the room. Silence. Total stillness. After a deep sigh, the Governess looked down at her feet and shook her head.

‘Disappointed...’ slowly, as she looked back up and raised her hand. Tony realised what was to happen.

‘My lady, ma’am, she is a young girl. She must be frightened. Let me go to her and help her. She has a brilliant mind, I can help her, let me...’

‘No’.

And with that final word, a shaft of light slashed through Tony. Without another word, his shocked expression morphed to sadness as he dropped to the ground, the blood from the wound slowly pooling around his lifeless form. Prudence took one last look at the floor before ordering the remaining two men to take away the body. ‘Those half breeds may hold the balance, but allowing me to be at the ceremony certainly had its advantages. That storm created quite a diversion.’ Prudence held her hand up once more, and the light that was radiating slowly dimmed. ‘Shame, I appear to have used too much magic. Never mind, we will have our day, but for now I need you all to stay focused, to be ready, and when the day comes for magic to return, do not step back from your chosen duties, from our rights.’

The whole group stood and applauded, showing their solidary to their coven.

Governess Prudence nodded once then turned towards the door to leave, her parting shot: 'Find her mother!' as she left the room.

Comfortable, warm but hungry, was the situation Milli now found herself in. She had brought all she needed but her money was dwindling, and she had realised that if she continued to use her card, she could be easily tracked. Milli needed to find another way of getting some cash. Retrospectively, she should not have used her card at all, and it bothered her slightly that nobody had followed the trail she had accidently left them. It was early morning, and the earth was warming with the rising sun. The wildlife stirring around her reminded Milli she had her own 'nature needs' to deal with. While settling herself into some sort of morning routine, her mind wandered. Every now and then she still got the thrill of awe at what she had become, but it was soon replaced by nervousness. Today though, she felt more in control and ready to act. She decided she would not head toward the quay side of Exeter as she had been there before but would go toward the cathedral area. She had seen pictures, heard tales and wanted to see it for herself - besides, being more central to the city, there might be more opportunities for work. Dressed, valuables in her pouch and ready to go, she raised her sunglasses to put them on, then paused. These had to go. They might have served as a fashion statement out in the holds, but here they stood out too much, and she felt they would lead to unwanted questioning. Putting them on for now though, she checked her surroundings and stepped away from her camouflaged home. Without thinking, and with what seemed like little effort, Milli turned around to leave and, with a sweep of her hand, vines closed over the opening, leaving the area looking like dense foliage.

Without thought, Milli had enjoyed the walk into the heart of the wilds. Her eyes had been darting everywhere, taking in all the sights, and her nostrils consumed the countless aromas. The difference between her home and this place was beyond comparison, but she still felt more at ease here than she ever did in Coventry. The thought of home made her heart retch as images of her parents and friends crossed her mind. Without thinking, she took her phone from her pouch and swiped the screen into life. '48% battery, and at this time everyone will be in class'. Her thoughts continued to muse over this while she began to wander up the main streets. Bustling activity increased around the shops and communal areas as she got closer to the cathedral. Just before the front of the garden steps, Milli caught sight of another leatherworker's stall, and an idea crossed her mind. Wandering over, she enquired about eye patches. The worker had been surprised by the request but went about looking for what he could possibly use to create the patch. She might have to show her eye once, but sometimes needs must for the bigger picture.

After the council meeting, it had taken the blue Water Walker Oroch, grey Air Walker Makkan and purple Portal Walker Lindany time to prepare to return to Exeter. They were feeling a little on edge about this next journey and unsure how to proceed if they found the girl. Makkan quietly felt she would be the best person to approach as she was also female, but Oroch had stepped in and pointed out that he was from Exeter and knew the people so he should be the one to approach her.

'With your pointy ears, you'll probably scare her off!' jested Lindany as they were gathering their final supplies.

'Lay off my ears, plum! Nobody looks at my ears!'

'And nobody calls me plum! Show a bit of respect or I'll send you to the depths of the Antarctic!' growled Lindany.

Makkan shook her head as the two sparred verbally with each other, but both were smiling so she was not concerned that a tsunami was going to be springing up any time soon. With a sweep of her hand, she raised the final supplies packages into the air, and with a bit of force, pushed them towards the two Walkers, so that they both 'oofed' as they took hold of the parcels.

'Ok Oroch, where to?'

The Water Walker thought about this for a time and then shrugged.

'Back to our base? At least we know it can hold a fire and there is safety coverage from the forest?'

The others couldn't think of a reason why not and agreed this was a good idea. Without another word, the world in front of them began to shimmer and split, the rippling haze widening until the portal had formed and the Walkers could step through. The three almost fell over each other as Oroch, who had gone first, had not walked forwards once he had passed onto Exeter soil.

'Oi…oh…' the annoyance had passed quickly as all beheld the sight in front of them.

'Someone's been busy,' commented Lindany as he stepped round Oroch and walked towards the home of vines. Walking round the dome and running his fingers lightly upon its surface, he eventually found the hanging vines that were covering up the entrance. His fingers slipped through their thin surface and parted the vines so all could look through. They all had to admit that the girl had done an excellent job. It was Lindany that pointed to the fire pit.

'Do you think she has mastered other elements then? I know Zyman has held the balance for other skills, but I have never seen him use…well, any of his skills!'

The others shrugged and stepping away from the house, they looked for other clues.

'Well, if nothing else, we can return here by nightfall and see her, but I would rather not let on that we have discovered this. It was a fortunate find, and who would have thought she would follow our path and find this place. Interesting. Maybe it has a significance, maybe not. But for now, let us go and look round Exeter. Keep all your senses open as our DragonSoul's might feel hers before we realise she is near.' The trio hid their possessions and headed off to the centre of Exeter.

Earth Walker Bechany and FireWalker Musany had not been out of Warwick since they had arrived and been greeted at the gates by the King. Their guides had gone and their guardian was now no longer on hand. Bechany very rarely thought of his home town of Cardiff, but on this journey, the pair had begun to reminisce. They soon realised that they had a love of music in common, with Cardiff being famous for its choirs and superb voices and Leeds being famous for its brass band works. Both holds boasted excellent colleges of music and arts scenes in general. It had passed the time well and had helped the pair to relax in each other's company enough that conversation had flowed smoothly, and they had grown closer.

'Imagine being part of those colleges, or those orchestras eh? It's not something that would happen in the wilds now, but the ruins of the colleges really stood out to me, their structure different from that around them. I read in history it was something to do with acoustics.'

'I hear you can still attend them if you are accepted but the reconstruction of the buildings is all virtual now...' The conversation stopped as the pair reached a crossroads. They glanced one way then the other and then sighed.

'Why couldn't Zyman have asked Milan or the other bloke to port us to Dorset before they went off? He just gave the orders in the wrong order I guess - Milan and Lindany already off organising.' He shrugged, sighed and a map was opened and a way chosen before the pair took up their conversation again.

Zyman had asked Milan to take them straight to the hotel room that the pair had been living in. Once through the portal, Zyman stood and took it all in, his eyes scanning the state of the bed, the used bathroom and the piles of magazines on the side table. His shoulders slumped and he moved, without energy, to the table where previously Governess Prudence had been sitting. He too began to finger the edges of the magazines but stopped and looked at Milan. He invited the Purple Walker to sit with him and before starting the conversation rose once more to order two cups of coffee from the room's service machine. Returning to the table, he placed the cups in front of each of them and smiled lightly at Milan.

'You harbour a heavy weight, and I'm concerned.' The leader of the Walkers stared at Milan with an intensity that made him squirm. Eventually Zyman looked down at his coffee and then slumped back in his chair. 'Eric looks more holder now than I have ever known him. He has always had a fascination with the other way of life: the only person I know to feel more comfortable on tarmac than dirt, more comfortable in a suit than….' He shook his head, to stop the flow of memories and looked back at Milan. 'Everybody forgets that he's my twin brother. We were both put forward to receive souls as nobody knew what would happen to the other, how they would feel if one was changed so. Yet here we are, and I know nothing of how my brother is feeling or doing. I worry about the council, I worry about my father, I am concerned for Eric. But I can't find answers for any of it!' He picked up the coffee up took a sip.

Milan, not sure where this conversation was going echoed the action but made no comment. 'I need to know he is ok. I need to know that his temper is not going to get the better of him without me there to support him, and I need his support...I need his drive.' Zyman's tone saddened, which was the final push Milan needed to speak openly and tell Zyman all that has been happening, his draconic iris widening as Zyman listened with a sense of growing concern. Finally, Milan reached the point he has been afraid to speak of.

'I think he believes he has only two choices open to him now, join the Governess or kill the girl.' Silence followed and Zyman sat like a stone. Milan felt his anger rising and continued with more force. 'He is your brother - you *need* to do something! He feels he has no place in the wilds any more as he is not a DragonWalker and never studied to take the throne, and you know the King would not favour him as heir, so where could he go? Would he be looked on with pity and descend into a simple existence? That is not Eric and you know it! Come over to the holds without chip, job, credential studies and work the slums? No. Zyman, he feels those are the two options open to him, and I can understand why. Why did you take so long to act!!??' The question burst out of Milan before he remembered who he was speaking to, but it shook Zyman enough for him to stop staring and admit the one thing that scared him the most.

'I didn't know what to do…'

Ex-Walker Steve and his now trusted friend had continued to head through Dorset. Steve had no idea why, but he felt he needed to get to Exeter and find this girl, but it was preying on his mind.

'You need to slow, Steve', his guide commented once they had stopped for something to eat and drink and to allow the horses time to recover. Steve frowned and shook his head. 'This is not the time to be worrying, we need to keep going...'

The guide shook his head and smiled.

'You're one tough old man, d'ya know that?!' He chuckled as Steve ended his sentence with

'..who is more annoyed that he still does not know how to weave baskets!' The pair continued with the light banter while they finished their meal.

'You know, this place is rather peaceful don't you think? They have some good ales, and keep themselves to themselves, but calm.' The guide nodded.

'I will be glad to get back onto known soil though, and we could have been there weeks ago if you had not wanted to sample each ale on offer!'

'Don't think I didn't notice you giving it a second opinion!' Old bones began to creak, and Steve slowly stood up. Leaning his weight on a stick he was using for support, he wandered over to his horse. Fussing the nose and patting the side of its face lovingly, he tried to get it to stop eating so that they could continue their journey. Suddenly, the horse whipped its head up and nipped slightly at Steve's arm. It was enough to knock him back onto his bottom. His friend was laughing as he walked over to try and help Steve up, while Steve was grumbling and calling his horse 'an old nag'.

This is how Steve and his guide were discovered by Bechany and Musany. They had been riding hard and caught up without realising it. Musany was off his horse like a shot and ran to offer help.

'What are you doing??!' Musany had not registered that the pair were laughing and jumped to the conclusion that the guide was attacking the old man. Steve and his friend looked up with such surprise and shock that Musany stopped in his tracks. His short stature meant that the sitting pair did not have to look up at him, but it took all of them a moment to register that Musany's short-cropped hair was smoking slightly. Bechany wandered over and placed a hand onto the firewalker's shoulder and smiled broadly.

‘I think we have found who we were looking for.’

# Chapter 14

# A Different Perspective

Eric left the restaurant in a foul mood. Milan had annoyed him, but not as much as the conversation with the Governess had confused him and the final words about Zyman upset him. Was his brother thinking of him at all? He knew nothing of the meeting that had subsequently followed, including Zyman coming to Coventry - not even of the death of Milli's father. He had shut himself off from everything and needed a diversion to get lost in; and the city's underbelly world was exactly where he would find it. It didn't take

Eric long to find a club offering all the VR out-of-body experiences that matched the drug-enhanced options used in the 1960s. He strode through the doors without hesitation but was taken aback by how clean the entrance area was - not unlike a hotel reception. Slowly surveying the entrance hall, Eric saw what looked like a manned reception area and went to inquire about the details. The very starched-suited receptionist took one look at him and raised his eyebrow.

'We don't often get Royal guests here, but at least I know you will be good for credit.' Eric's temper flared, and he almost slapped the man for his impudence. The receptionist waited patiently as he watched Eric rein in his temper, then he smiled. 'We offer nothing here but the indulgence of dreams. Your mind is a powerful place and every fantasy, every whim that has ever crossed your mind is in there. Our technology helps to amplify those desires so you can live them as you wish. Your every desire...' Eric cut him off.

'I get the idea, so less talking and get me plugged in.'

The receptionist nodded once and rose from his chair, beckoning the Royal to follow him.

Entering a vast space that brought to mind the Japanese pod hotels of the early 21st century, Eric and the Receptionist walked along row after row of occupied spaces until they reached an empty one. The receptionist went through the briefest of Health and Safety rules before adding,

'When you want to return, just call for an Exit. The command will shut down the machine and then deduct your time from your credit.'

Eric nodded his understanding and didn't listen to anything else the receptionist had to say. He failed to hear the quiet warning about not dwelling on a dream for too long or you ran the risk of forgetting about real living.

Four days later, Eric practically fell out of his pod, shaking, fatigued and looking very pale and very wide eyed. He stumbled up to the receptionist who smiled his knowing smile and handed Eric a restorative drink.

'This will see you home sir. Your retinal data can give you the coordinates of your hotel and I have deducted the substantial amount from your account.'

'Bastard!' Eric slurred as he weaved his way towards the exit, leaving the receptionist with a smirking smile. Eric had been mortified that he had been in the capsule for four days. He had had lovers, found fortune, lived the high cosmopolitan life, attended galas - but then things had started to change. He had lived out his whimsical desires before the deeper ones had surfaced - the face of the Governess swimming across his consciousness as he had re-witnessed the DragonSoul procession. The moment that finally had him running from the VR imagined council room and calling for an exit was his brother standing before him with half his soul being twisted into another form. The image had scared him back into the real world. Stumbling back to his hotel room had given Eric time to think, and he felt that maybe where his dreams had taken him was a way of helping him pick which outcome would best suit his life. It was clear that his mind was pushing him away from his brother, so joining the council here was a clear option. Who was he to think he could kill a DragonWalker?! Maybe this was why he was not chosen? Maybe the dragons foresaw that the life of a Walker was not his future? He needed to think more.

Natural Walker Zyman and Portal Walker Milan had arrived at the hotel and were concerned for the whereabouts of Eric, but the conversation that the two had been having had led to deeper discussions and they had not registered the time that had passed. As the Natural Walker had stood up to order some food to the room, speaking his order into the vending machine, he had wandered to look at the view of the metropolis outside. His mind unable to focus on the jarring images advertising sales and his draconic half seeming to baulk at the totally man-made environment surrounding it, Zyman continued to focus on the view.

'How do you stand it Milan? You have now been in Coventry for longer than any Walker in history, yet, you seem more comfortable in these surroundings than ever?'

Milan shrugged and went to join his friend by the window, his hands in his pockets after fidgeting with his unbuttoned collar.

'I feel no difference here than I do at home. I come and go between the two, and only when I have been uptight, have I found myself drawn to greenery...', his mind slipping back briefly to the small shop he had found himself standing outside of on the night he had stormed away from Eric and Prudence.

This was the scenario that Eric walked in on when he returned to the hotel room. His brother, in the clothes of the wilds, standing next to Milan, with the backdrop of Coventry through the window. It was a sight that stopped him in the doorway as they each slowly turned to face each other. Which brother was the most shocked at the change in the other was too close to call as they stood face to face; then both attempted to speak at the same time. For a moment, both Zyman and Milan expected Eric's temper to erupt, but he seemed to slump his shoulders; he didn't have the energy and was too deep in thought after his dreamscape binge. With what little strength he had left,

Eric raised his hand to allow Zyman to speak first. Zyman raised an eyebrow in surprise but spoke anyway.

'It is good to see you Eric. Whether you believe this or not, since your call to the castle I have been worried about you.'

Eric made no comment, his mind going over the conversation that ended with his brother doing nothing. He just said, 'You have changed' in unison with his brother. The brothers looked surprised and then looked down at themselves. It was a moment of harmony that made everyone laugh and eased the tense atmosphere by a few degrees. Milan decided to do the honours of ordering coffees as the brothers went to sit at the rooms single table that had been used time and time again. Zyman spoke first.

'It suits you…. You have changed, but I feel in more ways than just looks. Your look suggests a man who is making his way; you fit in here more than you ever did in the wilds.' Eric did his signature manoeuvre of running his fingers though his spiked hair before frowning and responding.

'I'm not so sure about you though, brother. You look tired and older than your years and what's with the extended scales?'

This made the Walker frown and stand in order to view his reflection in the mirror. His hand raised to his face, and he traced the scales slowly drifting towards his neckline. His eyes shot to Milan before back to the mirror. He did not say another word but slowly unbuttoned his shirt. Once he had removed it, his toned, trim torso still looked the same until he turned his back to them. Shimmering across his skin were the scales that had started on his shoulder as just a small patch. Now they covered his entire back, the area accenting the starting of ridges that were protruding from his back. The scales running over Zyman's shoulder blades were well-defined and a deep shade of green but gradually blended with his own skin down the back of his arms. He didn't say a word before slipping his shirt back on and turning to Eric and Milan.

'We have been putting it down to working hard with the balance. Nobody has managed to find any record of this happening to previous Walkers, and I never saw any of our immediate elders with such markings. Each one of us is being affected differently. Nobody has been affected on their face or hands - so we have been able to continue doing our duties, but it's as though the harder we have to work, the more draconic we become.' Zyman took a breath. He realised that he was opening up in a way that he always shied away from, but he felt that Eric needed to hear this. Zyman also needed this; he needed Eric to understand that he needed him. Why he couldn't come out and just say that, he was not sure. But, somewhere in his mind, he hoped Eric would register that his brother was trusting him. 'Oroch has been effected the worst, and I am glad that Makkan fell in love with the man before his changes; she has been such a support, but it is as if he had to prove himself so much that he overdid things to excess. He hides it well, but I know it bothers him greatly. We hold what we call 'the balance', we support the wilds any way we can, be it advice, guidance or magic, and we have become stronger than we could ever have imagined, but the strain on our bodies is beginning to take its toll. I have found no written details of such a...' Zyman stopped and turned to Milan. The Purple Walker took a step back and, in that instant, the two just stood and stared at each other and made the same realisation which Milan confirmed with a surprised tone in his voice.

‘I have not changed at all!’ He looked from Eric to Zyman and then to his own hands, holding them up for scrutiny.

‘I have been in the holds supporting Eric for much of my time. I returned to the wilds on occasions when called or when in need of some thinking time, but other than that we have been here. I have been using my magic as much as anyone the only difference is I have not entered the council room to meditate. We have travelled freely through Coventry using my portals.’ For a moment everyone looked at each other before Zyman slumped back into his chair.

‘More riddles, and still the DragonSouls don’t really talk. It rather crept up on us, our souls gradually becoming silent as we continued to work. We all felt it was to give us the control in this lifetime, but as this silence has crept up, nobody has really registered it. I get the odd flash of their emotions when they feel we are threatened, and on occasions when seeking their council, they have spoken about if they feel it's the right course of action, but other than that...'

Milan agreed. 'I feel like my soul is not really there. It's as if he slumbers most of the time, leaving me in control... as if... it's as if he has given up.' This did stir Milan's DragonSoul and a sadness washed over Milan that made his knees crumple; his hands covered his face as tears welled in his eyes. The overwhelming feeling of being lost and alone was like a tsunami that wouldn't stop, crashing against his psyche repeatedly as he felt himself falling into the depths of this sorrow. He heard Zyman shouting his name and felt Eric holding onto his hand, anchoring him just before he was lost. Gradually, he rose from the depths of anguish his mind was taking him into. He came gasping to the surface, saying over and over that he didn't know what that was, what was happening, and then it was gone. Milan rose from the floor and straightened his clothes and then frowned. 'Gone...'.

The trio sat in silence for some time before Zyman updated his brother on everything that had been happening, everything they had done and how close they felt they were to Milli.

As Eric listened to his brother with mixed emotions, it dawned on him that Zyman had not forgotten him, but still, his decision had been made and no time like the present to explain. Looking at his brother with a sad smile, he finally uttered the words that he never thought he would ever admit to.

'I am sorry, John I have misjudged you for so long that it had become a bitter part of myself, only now do I realise that you and the group have not ostracised me, and I have been a fool to think you had. I cut off father; I have not returned home. But, with all that said and done, I have made my decision, and I hope you will respect it. I have been offered a place on Coventry's council, and I am going to accept. Governess Prudence has been gracious in her hospitality, and we have had more freedom to move around here than we should. Milan has been my dearest friend and will continue to be, but I doubt the council will accept a DragonWalker into their ranks - imagine the political backlash that would create with the other holds on this island! I feel it will be bad enough that I am a Royal wilder. Because of this, Milan, I thank you for everything you have done, but you need to go back now and continue your work. The other Walkers will need your help, and I won't beholden you to me any longer'.

Milan did not talk about the tightness in his chest that Eric's words caused, but, looking sad, he did not argue; nor did Zyman, who simply stood up and walked to stand beside Eric. Eric rose out of habit and the brothers embraced. It was a tender moment filled with love and respect. Stepping away from each other, the brothers continued to look at each other with faces showing an array of emotions. With that passing moment, a shimmering portal opened behind Zyman, it hovered there showing the gates of Warwick castle in its hazy form. The two Walkers stepped through it and were gone.

*Nobody was aware of the glimmer of life that was beginning to form around the DragonSoul Stone. Its shimmering surface rippling with an inner light so faint it was almost imagined.*

Though Milli, and the three in pursuit, were all within Exeter, they seemed to be leading each other a merry dance. Lindany could not understand why they did not just try and catch her at her makeshift home, but the other two emphasised that if they did that, it would scare her away and then she could go anywhere. They checked each morning that she had been home, and, because the signs of habitation continued, they searched for her within the wilds during the day. Rumours of a healer of great effect had begun to circulate within the wilds: a nurse, medically trained but with an amazing success rate at curing all ailments without the expense of medication. The trio had overheard this while having an evening meal at the local inn. Oroch was the first to speak as he noted that now they know how she was making money, but why was nobody coming forward and speaking of her as a Walker? Surely that was how she was healing them, and the three of them were not hiding their draconic eyes from the world. After this discussion, the three drifted into a comfortable silence, each deep in their own thoughts. Makkan had been holding her drink up in front of her and with a glazed look was looking through the window into the street. The passers-by seemed comfortable with the Walkers' presence, busily going about their lives, their trades, or sitting, as the Walkers were, enjoying the calm atmosphere about them. She had realised that they lived a slower life down here than what they had become used to in Warwick and, it reminded Makkan of her home town of Truro. Shaking herself out of her reverie, she turned to look at Oroch and reached out her hand and took his. Drawing it closer to her, she began to turn his hand over to look at the scales that caught the light as his hand was moved. His nails were still human but looked strange in the hand that was almost draconic. The Blue Walker followed her gaze to his hand and gave a light shrug.

'It doesn't feel any different than it did before, it's just strange that it doesn't go back to normal now.'

His tone was light, but he looked sad. Lindany was about to chip in but saw a strange look in the Air Walker's expression and, deciding that this was a moment where three was a crowd, he vacated. Lindany left saying he was going to wander to other social areas and listen for more information on the interesting healer. Oroch and Makkan didn't really listen to him as they both knew where this moment was heading: they had been walking this path for a long time. Makkan continued to run her fingers over the blue scaled hand before turning it back over so it was palm up. Oroch closed his fingers around her hand, but she did not resist. She looked up at him and smiled. With her free hand, she went to move some hair out of his eyes to behind his pointed ears. Oroch didn't want any attention focused on his ears so his free hand went to stop her. They ended up in a slightly strange embrace. Neither of them moved, but eventually Oroch smiled lightly and, with Makkan echoing his smile, Oroch leaned forward and kissed her. It was very delicate at first, almost hesitant but, when the Air Walker responded, the kiss became firmer and the love and respect that he had been feeling toward Makkan exploded, releasing a torrent of emotions that had been growing between them since their first camping outing, many moons ago. As if synchronised, they rose from their table, drinks forgotten, and wandered deeper into the inn. Still holding on to each other's hands, they requested a room. They looked at each other with nervous anticipation as it was confirmed a room was free. As the key was handed over to them, they quickly took their leave, their passion finding its release in the privacy of those four walls.

Lindany wandered to and fro in different parts of the central section of Exeter, but nothing really seemed to be going on. For the first time since becoming the Purple Walker, he felt a little out of place. He had nothing really to do at the time and, in fairness, he was glad to have his own council for a while. Sitting on the lawn in the shade of the cathedral, he watched people passing by. Some people walked with purpose, others wandered while talking, some eating, some drinking. It was very relaxing. He watched a young girl wearing an eye patch go into a shop, then exit with some bottles of strange liquid, which he wanted to ask her about. He watched a young man carry a length of material into the tailor store. His eyes wandered back to the girl with the eyepatch and he pondered on what had befallen her that she felt she had to cover her face. He admired her dress and the slenderness of her waist and then looked back to her face. Lindany couldn't escape the confusion he felt as the girl walked away from him. He felt anger at the thought that someone may have hurt the girl resulting in what Lindany surmised was a bruised eye. He felt curious; he wanted to introduce himself and maybe offer to help carry her bottles. All these thoughts caught him off guard but, shaking his head, he chuckled, thinking internally that he had been spending far too long with Oroch and Makkan and thinking of those two; he hoped that they had finally come together in union so that he could stop watching them dance around each other. As the young girl walked out of his view, Lindany's thoughts turned back to his current situation, and he decided that he would return home for some food and quiet back in the council chamber.

Lindany returned to the council chamber and was surprised to see the four Walkers sitting round a table eating a meal when they should be in the council halls holding the balance. He wandered over to them and, with a smile of welcome, joined them for their meal.

‘Are you that confident with holding the balance now, you can do this anywhere?’ Lindany asked, looking at them in turn. It was the Air Walker Siska who answered for the group as he shook his head.

‘No, not at all. Zyman returned from the holds recently and has given us a break. His strength is off the chart, but he is holding the balance for all of us right now. He said he needed to meditate on his thoughts and could hold the elements at the same time.’ The conversation centred on all that had been going on while the Walkers ate, but then Lindany decided it was time to go and see Zyman before returning to his task. As he got up from the table, he looked back at Siska and smiled.

‘Grey hair and eyes suit you, you know!’

The Air Walker chuckled and agreed that he thought so too. As Lindany walked away, he left them to conversations about looks and their home towns.

Lindany was quiet and respectful as he entered the DragonWalker council room and saw Zyman sitting in the centre. He was a striking figure to behold as he sat there with his legs crossed, his back straight and his hands resting on his knees, palms down. Zyman had his top stripped bare and Lindany could see the light shimmering off his muscled back. Zyman did not open his eyes but he smiled, his elongated canine teeth appearing slightly sinister.

'It is good to see you my friend. Once the others have finished eating and return to their duties, I will gladly join you for some food myself. Milan is here also - perhaps he would like to join us. It would be good for you two to catch up as I think he could use a friendly ear right now.'

Lindany nodded. Zyman took a moment to stretch, his long strawberry blond hair brushing his shoulders and adding contrast to the striking green of his skin. He let out a deep breath and sighed.

'Before you go, answer me this. Do you feel ok?'

It took Lindany a moment to think about this before he smiled. 'Never better. Fit, healthy and strong'.

The sitting DragonWalker nodded and returned his attention to the balance.

Milli had picked up the iodine liquid she needed from the store near the cathedral and headed back toward the open tracks. Her journey to the hospital site never took her long on foot but nevertheless, she enjoyed the time alone. She and Yebby often looked at the sights and discussed everything that they saw and felt. Often, Milli would allow a little of her magic to flow, enabling small buds to rise up, sapling trees to extend their growth, but always with a delicate touch.

'We are getting better!' she would comment to her soul, to which her draconic half would radiate its pride. Over the time they had been together, a very strong bond had developed and they now lived for each other and looked out for each other. Milli found that they could talk while she was awake in a pictorial emotional way, but she enjoyed it most when she had time to relax her mind and join her dragon soul in conversation. They were a team and worked well together, each one being able to read the other without fear of being questioned. Often, when Milli was unsure of her choices at the hospital, her soul would resonate with courage, or, if she was nervous, she would feel a calmness wash over her. As she was leaving the shop today, she had felt a strange nervousness, as if she was being watched, but Yebby had shown no sign of concern so she had dismissed it on the walk as her own nervousness creeping in. Since finding a small job at the hospital, as a cleaner, she had enjoyed delicately using her skills to help ease a wound or mend a break. She had found ways of doing this without the dramatics of what had happened at Warwick, and Yebby did not mind that she kept the one eye covered with the patch. That had been a stroke of genius, and Milli had walked about Exeter freely ever since finding the leather worker. Today her routine was going to be slightly different. She had heard of some women who had come in with some burns. She had not worked with burns before but realised that she could control all elements, to a point, and she was eager to see if she could ease a burn.

Steve, his guide and the two DragonWalkers had spent time exchanging news and laughed frequently about how they had met. Steve continued to say that due to his age he needed to stop regularly for ale supplements, but in truth, they all knew they were listening out for news regarding what was going on. It was getting frustrating that nothing was being said about the lost Walker, no further signs of magic being used - in fact, no news of anything other than the day-to-day lives of the people around them. Both the Earth and Fire Walkers often stopped to help where they could, if people approached them to ask, but it was always simple fixture-and-fitting type jobs. They wondered what was happening with the others, but they could do nothing about it at this time. Steve had shown that he knew nothing of what was happening to them - nothing other than what they had all read - and no other ways of locating the Natural Walker. They had decided to stick together and finish Steve's journey, for no other reason than they were not sure how to proceed.

# Chapter 15
# The Truth

*The DragonSoul Stone had begun to shake as the energy within increased. The light rippled across the stone, the metallic walls of its prison making it look larger than life and the vibrations intensified with each passing moment.*

After watching Milan and his brother leave, Eric spent some time looking at the view from his window before making the decisive steps to the start of his new life. On texting Governess Prudence, she confirmed that he could meet her at her office and that transport would be arranged. He gathered up his belongings, checked around the room for anything forgotten or out of place, and then switched off the light and closed that chapter of his life. By the time Eric reached the hotel lobby, a car had come to a halt outside the entrance, the digital display running the length of the vehicle registered that the taxi was for him. On placing his hand on the door scanner plate to verify him as the authenticated rider, the car door opened. Eric looked back once more before entering the vehicle then sat back while the car sped him to his destination.

Oroch and Makkan had left the inn and meandered round the cathedral area looking for Lindany. It hadn't taken them long to realise what had probably happened, so they took the time to sit on the lawn and look down towards Oroch's family home, being the cathedral. The lawn and old steps leading the DragonWalkers' eyes towards the main entrance, along with the beautiful stained-glass window which still caught the day's light after so many years. They had visited that morning and helped Oroch's mother with some of her morning chores before heading off to look for Milli. Makkan had become very fond of the lady and both had quietly talked about their feelings for Oroch. Makkan knew that his mother's womanly instincts would notice that something had changed between the Walkers, but she herself wanted to cheer from the rooftops, so that was not going to be a hardship. As they walked down the street, at first Oroch had shied away from the brief moments when Makkan had brushed her hand against his, overcoming his concern for the scales on his hand had helped him to finally accept her touch and the pair sat hand in hand in the cathedral's grounds. The previous evening, as they had lain on the bed talking, Makkan had pointed out the changes to Oroch's leg as well as his hand, but he had complained of no pain, and the respect he felt for Makkan that she accepted him like this had only affirmed their love for each other. The stories they shared of their time as Walkers, as well as learning everything that made each other tick, had helped them to form the relationship they both now realised they had. Sitting in the grounds of the cathedral and being so focused on each other, had stopped time meaning anything, and they completely forgot their focus for the day.

As Eric's car finally reached the Governess's office, he felt the first twinge of trepidation. What was he going to do? Could he request a place to live? He entered the foyer of the shard of metal that rose up from the centre of Coventry. Everything was automated, and he was directed to the nearest lift which he entered. He pressed no buttons but stared at himself in the mirrored walls of the elevator cabin; while it swiftly rose up the floors. His hands went to sort his spiked hair, which had drooped slightly; he needed a haircut! He straightened his three-piece suit, then his shoulders and flexed his neck from side to side. His eyes focused on his reflection, and he tried out a few different expressions before shaking his head and turning to face the door that would be his exit. The lift stopped and the doors opened on a vast room with a beautiful oval table in the centre. The table was showing all the usual news feeds and social media coverage across its surface, but he was surprised to see more data sliding across the glass windows, obscuring the view for but a moment before it moved off the screen to be filled with more information. One lady was sitting to the side of the room. She rose, her sharp suit matching her features as she walked over to Eric.

'You should not be here. You should have stayed at home. This is no place for someone from the wilds...!' She was cut off mid-sentence as the double doors to the room opened and Prudence, accompanied by her entourage, filed into the room and took up their places. The look the lady got from Prudence was enough to make anyone quake. She bowed to Prudence, straightened her shoulders and began to leave.

'I would watch your tongue if I we're you my dear. Your husband doesn't want to see you with him too soon now does he? Hmmm?' Prudence chuckled and sighed. 'Parents of important children should know their place', reminding everyone in the room that the only reason the lady was still here was because she was Milli's mother. With no grace but with purpose, Prudence turned toward

Eric and clapped her hands together. The bangles that encircled her wrists tinkled in the silence that followed.

'You came. And you have decided to join us?'

Prudence's tone, as always, demanded some sort of response, so Eric nodded slightly. They looked at each other before Eric was given a sharp smile and the Governess headed towards the ranks of people sitting around the table.

'Ladies and gentlemen of Coventry, this timing could not be any better. The young Royal Eric has decided to finally join us on the day we are off to kill his brother.'

Nobody spoke but then a few began to clap and eventually the whole audience was giving a standing ovation.

'Hang on, hang on, what?!?!'

'No time to change your mind young Eric. I have been clear from the start that we would take measures to help you get your soul, have I not? You have just been focusing on the wrong one. What better soul to have than the one your brother has bonded with? You are twins, the transition should be fine! What am I saying? We have no intention of getting the soul from your bother.'

'But the killing bit?'

'Yes, I meant that part. And all the other Walkers that have stolen our right from us. Brothers and sisters of Coventry, have we waited long enough for our right to share in the magic of this world? Since those decaying, rotting dragons found a way to syphon magic to rebuild themselves, we have had to replace our magic with technology. Transport, communications, mass mindlessness of a population within our holds. It has all been to prepare us for the day magic returns, and that day is coming. No, it is here!'

Eric was stunned and just stared at Prudence. For a time, his eyes glanced over the data on the window and he realised they were figures on nothing he had ever seen before and had no idea of their origin. He couldn't take that in as well as what Prudence had said so stumbled over a few words to give himself time.

'Syphon magic? Keep the balance you mean?'

'Please Eric. It would take a very simple and naive human to believe they could hold the elements of the world in balance. No, the balance of the elements holds itself, and it does a fine job I might add. No, all you have been doing is syphoning magic from the elements to build up the dragons' magic so that when the day came, they could be reborn as the majestic creatures they once were. So maybe I should rephrase my earlier sentence: the day the *dragons* kill your brother.'

Eric's world spun and he began to pace the room.

'You're wrong! The Walkers hold the balance. They keep the peace and help the Wilds.' As Eric spoke, the realisation that twelve people could not possibly do all the work that was needed to sustain all the different areas began to turn over in his mind. How? They were able to work in teams.

'No, you're still wrong Prudence, the elements...'

Prudence sighed and wandered over to get herself a drink from the slim bar at the far side of the room. It was as though it was only her and Eric in the room and they had forgotten the audience around the table.

'Yes, the elements. "Each dragon controls an element." That is the wrong wording, and it is what you have missed for as many generations as you care to go back. They do not control them; they can draw on them, they can work with them, and, I guess, okay, they *can* control them, but the forces of nature are far stronger in this world and cannot be controlled. Your Water Walkers do not tell it to rain across the country; your Fire Walkers to not tell a volcano when to erupt; but they can stem its flow or reduce its power. Do you see? The dragons were dying; they slumbered for too long seeking their wisdom and, in that time, we witches, wizards and warlocks grew stronger and developed our own understanding of magic. It was a bountiful time for us, and though humans hunted us through the ages, they never realised how much they relied on us. Humans have lived in a world where they don't need the balance, where their minds can function in VR as much as in the real world, where they can get all they need at their fingertips. You see?'

'But the wilds…' stammered Eric with more and more concern showing in his rapid movements and clipped tone.

'Yes, well, we were unable to touch the wilds. Although the dragons were using people to get their magic back, they had worked it in such a way that the history around them protected them. People do like their traditions, their histories...'. She paused to give Eric time to argue, but he had nothing he could say so she continued. Raising her glass, she smiled her sinister smile.

'It was only through seeing the changes between you and your brother that we realised the signs were there - the subtle differences since the procession and the joining of John and his soul Zyman, and you without your soul. We could not have wanted for a better comparison. Most helpful, thank you'. Prudence took a sip of her drink and added, 'While you have been so focused on keeping the balance, doing good deeds, and searching for the Natural Walker, none of you have felt the magic building; seen the signs all around you that magic is ready to come into the world once more; blind to the subtle changes of power that have been happening. And now... and now the Magic is back!'

Prudence stopped talking then and clicked her fingers. A small circle of purple light filled her hand and she smiled broadly. Slowly, each person around the table stood up and did the same, the orbs they were all holding now filling the office with an eerie violet hue. Each one of them held their hand forward and the glowing orbs seemed to expand. ‘Purple Walkers held ether magic, yes? The ability to transcend space. I feel it is time we used this magic to visit Warwick, do you not agree?’

Eric had no idea what was about to happen, but running was the only thing that he could think of doing. The Governess seemed to have completely forgotten that he was there, and he was going to use that to his advantage. He ran from the hall to the lift, cursing it for its lack of speed. The doors opened but he almost backed away as the bitter lady who had spoken to him previously was standing in there. She grabbed him and pulled him into the lift before he could get away and pressed the button for the ground floor. It was a long way and gave her time to ask a simple question.

‘Is Milli alive?’

When Eric did not answer, she shook him and asked again. When he responded that she was and that she was in Exeter not Warwick, the lady seemed openly relieved.

'They killed my husband for not doing his job properly. They tolerate me as I am her mother. I love Milli. Please tell her so if you get to her. And you must get to her, please! Listen closely Eric of Warwick. Milli is not a witch so do not fear her. I am not a witch either, my husband was a warlock and we met when I was already pregnant by another. He took me in when I was at my lowest, and he was a good man. I wonder now how much of that was planned by Her Highness Prudence, but his love for me became real. He loved Milli as his own and he has died for that fact.' She would have said more but the doors of the lift opened.

'Run Eric. Use your phone...' and with that, she turned and walked in the opposite direction.

Eric's mind had been in such a spin that he had forgotten about the phone he had been given. At this point he didn't care if it was being tracked. He would use it and dump it. He just hoped Milan still had his phone, for old times' sake.

Zyman, Milan and Lindany had made their way down to Ray's inn and were enjoying a peaceful moment when a variety of things happened at once. Lindany suddenly stood up and looked around as several vast portals opened and closed, as if the power had suddenly burst from him. Zyman grasped his head and collapsed to the ground, and Milan's phone started ringing. For a moment, Milan was too busy shaking Zyman's shoulder, trying to get an answer out of the man, but his mind also registered that only one person would ring the number of the phone he had been clinging onto just in case. Stepping away from Zyman and Lindany, he answered the phone. Eric's voice sounded desperate and he was breathing hard, trying to talk while running.

'Milan, you need to come and get me. We have got to get to Exeter. Get away from Warwick. The dragons are coming....'

At that precise moment, as Eric uttered those words, Zyman turned to face Eric with eyes no longer mismatched, and canines now protruding from an elongating muzzle.

Steve and his good friend were back on the road and didn't mind being joined by the others. They had no further updates but were very close to Exeter now and all were looking forward to a good meal. His guide had begun telling them stories of Exeter's streets and the descriptions of the cobbled areas and the quay. It had piqued the interest of the quartet, and they were looking forward to seeing the place. All four of them had come to appreciate the skills of Lindany and Milan with almost a reverence because of the time it had taken them to walk and ride. They admitted to themselves they could have done it quicker but, with no apparent urgency and accepting that Steve knew nothing more of what was happening, it had turned into a pleasant, but long experience. While they were travelling, Steve began to feel a little uneasy, as if something was tugging at his mind and making him rethink everything he knew. He felt like he should be doubting himself without any understanding of why. Suddenly Bechany and Musany shouted out in pain, clinging to their heads and falling from their steeds. Fire erupted where Musany had landed, and he looked as though he was engulfed in fire and smoke. Bechany staggered about, turning this way and that as if tormented by unseen spirits. The pair were oblivious to Steve asking what was wrong when suddenly the guide grabbed his friend around his waist and pulled him back.

'I don't like this... Let's go....'

Steve could not take his eyes from the image in front of him, of his friend being consumed in flames - while his other friend was disappearing in a swirling sandstorm. Their cries had stopped, and they became calmer. Steve could not believe the shapes he was seeing in the shadows, now and it took a lot for the guide to pull him away.

'We need to get out of here.'

Milli had finished her shift at the hospital and had been exceptionally pleased with the outcome of her burns experiment. She was able to take the heat out of the burn and then, using some of the water elements, had been able to rehydrate the area ready for the skin to heal itself naturally. She smiled to herself and commented to Yebby that it would be just another rumour regarding the amazing medicine of Exeter. As she came to the end of the track and approached the centre of Exeter, she sighed and, with Yebby's permission, replaced her eye patch and became one more Exeter citizen once more. Her cloak going around her shoulders helped her to blend in even more. Milli was walking through the centre of the city when the cries of the people around her suddenly turned into terror and shock. People were screaming as they ran away from the giant dragons in the sky. Milli looked skyward and could not believe what she saw; a dragon of pillar-box red and another of a murky brown were circling the sky trumpeting their deep cries as fire erupted from one's mouth while the other seemed to be whipping up a storm with its wings. Milli backed away and in her mind, so did Yebby - the souled pair not sure what to do or what to think. Suddenly, she heard a cry as a young boy fell sprawled out in front of her. She helped him up, checked he was ok and let him go. This act drew her attention back down to city level, rather than up at the skies, and her eyes went wide with shock. A few buildings had been reduced to rubble, but other buildings were ablaze; the fire was spreading fast from building to building, travelling along the vines that connected them. As she continued to scan the scenario playing out in front of her, Milli was enthralled by the sight of two DragonWalkers engaging with the dragons, and the feeling that she must help overwhelmed her.

Oroch and Makkan were standing at the end of the street with their hands raised. Milli realised that one of the Walkers was controlling the wind and trying to stop the sandstorms from decimating the area. But what the other Walker was doing was phenomenal; he was transforming! His hands were outstretched, his legs buckled the wrong way as they completed their full draconic look. The claws of his feet dug grooves into the ground as he held his place against the elements. He was totally focused on drawing together the clouds around him, bringing water to each fire as fast as he could by using rain. With Musany still flying around spewing fire with each breath, Oroch was using more and more of his magic to calm the fires being caused.

He cried out suddenly as the material of his top ripped and protruding from his shoulder burst a wing with its membrane still forming. Makkan grabbed at him then, calling his name, shouting for him, to stop but Oroch wouldn't listen and, through gritted teeth said that he couldn't let this happen to his home.

Without thinking, Milli joined the DragonWalkers and said,

'let me help!' She didn't think about how she would help or what an untrained Walker could do compared to the power that these two were wielding but she did what she could, calling on nature to run soil over smouldering ground and new growth to shore up rooftops where walls were becoming unstable.

Makkan simply exclaimed

'You!' before turning back to the tasks in hand.

The dragons flying in the sky did not care about the damage they were doing below. To them, they were free and enjoying the feeling of the wind under their wings, stretching claws to the sky and exulting their joy to the world. The power rippling through their muscles as they began to duck, dive and roll would have been something to behold if people weren't running and trying to take cover. As the dragons soared to a great height and moved on, Oroch, Makkan and Milli, were able to get some sort of semblance of order to the area they were working on. The residents of Exeter began to settle and tend to their homes, shops and belongings. The three stood with brows sweating and limbs shaking and stared at each other. Makkan spoke up and thanked Milli for her help. Makkan was about to say more, but her attention was focused on her lover with panic in her eyes. He was standing beside them with his clothes in shreds where spines were protruding from his back, one wing keeping his balance, leaning slightly on legs which bent the wrong way from the knee joint. The pain in his expression indicated he was fighting something the others could not understand. Makkan was distraught and didn't know what to do for the best. She placed her hands about his face, touched his chest, his arms, all the time mumbling his name and asking what was going on. When Milli opened her mouth, it was not her voice that was heard. For the first time since the dragon souls had been paired, Yebby spoke.

'He is becoming Oroch the Dragon. The man is fighting it. His thoughts are in turmoil for you and he is worried that you will get hurt. The dragons above you worked with the balance for a long time - standing in the council room and focusing on their element for a lot longer than you have, as you have been away working in the wilds. Oroch pushed himself to use more and more magic so he is more advanced than you, but the same will happen to you. Your DragonSoul will come to the fore, and you will be lost.'

With that, Milli was back and looking blankly at the Air Walker. Makkan was about to say more when Oroch cried out and crumpled to his knees. His hands found those of Makkan but all she could do was step back as she watched the second wing burst through the remains of Oroch's shirt, which finally fell away to reveal his whole body covered in scales. His torso and legs swelled and extended. His eyes were closed, but his lower face was more of a muzzle dappled with whiskers and a lot of very sharp teeth. As the other two DragonWalkers continued to back away, Oroch twisted and turned as he grew. Finally, with a trumpet of joy and the bursting of what seemed like a funnel of water, he stretched his sinuous neck, opened his sail-like wings and, beating them steadily, rose into the sky for his maiden flight. The sun caught the brilliance of his scales, his tail whipping left and right to steer him onto the air currents lifting him higher and higher as he headed off in search of the other two dragons that had left the area.

# Chapter 16
# The Mist Speaks

Milan was frozen in time as he watched Zyman and Lindany's bodies twist, turn, alter and morph into beasts of purple and green. He had slowly backed away, but his eyes were still focused on the spot where he had seen Zyman's face distort into a muzzle just moments ago. Now his vision was filled with the vast forms of two stunning dragons. They had not taken flight but were sitting on their haunches, stretching their sinuous necks towards the sky and trumpeting with ear-shattering noise. Their wings unfurled to reveal a membrane which seemed to ripple with the dominant colour and white as the light struck the new surface. Zyman was bigger than his purple brother, but together they filled the street. The dragons were oblivious to the damage their tails were causing as they whipped back and forth. Their front legs were held high as they pawed the air in preparation for flight. Milan stood petrified, looking at his own hands and back to the dragons before him with fear etched into his every feature. One hand still held his phone, and he could hear his name being shouted out repeatedly with more and more anger. He was not sure if it was he who responded or his DragonSoul, but suddenly a portal opened in front of him and Eric fell through it, hitting the dirt and rolling to a stop at the foot of the great green dragon. Eric was dazed and unable to move for what seemed to be some considerable time. He then shook his head and rolled onto his front to get up onto his knees. The sight of his friend being so close to the elongated claws shocked Milan into action, and he ran forward to pull Eric out of the way. As he was dragging Eric backward, the green dragon made one final sweep with his eyes before launching into the air. The take-off was not delicate as the wingbeats were uncoordinated, his body wobbling with uncertainty like a young cygnet trying out its wings for the first time. As he gradually brought his wings under control and gained altitude, the green dragon grew in confidence. Lindany took one last look at the ground, snapped his great jaw at an overturned cart and snarled as one of his wings caught the roof of a nearby building. As he recovered, his attention was caught by Milan and Eric struggling to put as much distance between themselves and the two dragons as they could, and he lowered his muzzle. Lindany let out another grumble, but this was in response to the confusion he experienced as he became conscious of the DragonSoul within Milan. At the same time, the sorrow that had overwhelmed the Purple Walker in Coventry washed over him again but not with so much force. Shaking to control this emotion, Milan watched as Lindany tilted his head slightly to one side.

Scrabbling to get away, Eric and Milan finally got to their feet and ran as fast as they could towards the massive gates of Warwick castle. Almost falling over each other to get behind the protective gates, they were met with as much chaos on the inside as on the outside. People were running everywhere, but a solo figure in the centre caught their eye.

'Father!' Eric cried and ran to the King. He was shocked by the reception as his father engulfed him in a strong hug and the King held his son for many long moments before he looked up and registered Milan. Stepping quickly around Eric, his hands reached for Milan's throat and gripped him with vice-like force.

'Why not you? What have they done to my son? What is happening? Tell me, damn you Walker!'

Eric raised a hand and placed it on his father's shoulder as Milan stumbled over his words, stating over and over that he did not know. His mismatched eyes pleading with the King to understand. The King did not let go of Milan's neck, but turned his head to Eric, feeling the touch of his son's hand on his shoulder. The young Royal composed himself in a way his father never thought he would see from his hot-tempered son. The scene held for a moment, then Eric began to speak. He was honest as he explained about his dealings with Prudence, his decisions, his deluded view of his brother; but finally, he finished with what was happening outside.

'For all these years the dragons have been fooling us father. They have been drawing on the balance to gain strength in their magic, to bring themselves back from death and live again within the magic. The balance is just a word they used to fool us and give them time to syphon the elements.' His tone was sobering before he added, 'The metallic holds harbour all the witches and warlocks. They banded together waiting for the magic to return - hoping for a time when dragons would not steel their magic and would allow them to be who they truly are. The dragons have been taking for themselves since the myths became legends. They lost themselves in the wisdom of time but found a way to get their bodies back.' Eric paused for a moment to send an apologetic look to Milan before he continued. 'They have killed our Royal blood lines; they don't care for man and all we have done is feed off their stories, believed their lies and, helped them with their return.'

The King finally let go of Milan and took a deep sigh before looking about the room. Eric had not finished though, and he added;

'The witches and warlocks have got their power back and are on their way here. I don't know what they will do, but Governess Prudence, their leader, is not someone I would trust again.'

The King nodded once then walked toward the open gates to look outside. What he saw turned his stomach as parts of his beloved Warwick were destroyed and the people were running in panic.

'We need order here. We need a plan of action.' He turned to Milan then. 'Are you with them or willing to help us?! Answer fast, Milan.'

The shaken Walker looked at his hands for a long time before covering his face and closing his eyes.

'I don't feel like my DragonSoul is taking me over. I am in control. I will help in any way I can.'

A dark shadow fell across the area where they stood, and all knew that one of the dragons had begun to circle around the castle, the trumpeting sound being echoed by another, and then more joined in, in the far distance. Everyone knew it meant the other dragons were almost upon them. It spurred the king into action, and he began barking orders to protect the castle, to get people to safety. He stopped and turned to Eric and Milan, who had been trailing in his wake.

'You did not spend any time here, Milan, and I think that is why you are slow to change, but I warn you that I think you will. Any signs of change and you will be locked up without hesitation.'

The King paused for moment, his fingers holding the bridge of his nose as he frowned and thought. 'The other missing Walker is the only other one who has spent no time with the balance. Get her back here now.' The King's voice was harsh as he continued. 'The last Reports were that the three Walkers who went after the girl found where she lived but had not let on as they did not want her to run again.' A small pause in the conversation as all looked grimly at each other. Finally, the King added 'The time for running is over, and she has more power than any of you, and while she still can, we need her skills. Enough time has been wasted trying to be nice. Get her here and I will protect this land for as long as I can.'

Eric and Milan nodded, turned on their heels and ran into a portal conjured by Milan.

Milli had finally pulled her eyes away from Oroch and was trying desperately to console Makkan, who was on her knees screaming for her beloved. The Natural Walker had no idea what to do or say, but getting the girl to move seemed like the logical thing to do.

'They have gone. We need to go!'

Makkan took a lot of persuading, and eventually, Milli had to almost drag her to move. She had no idea where to go or where to run to, but the only place that came to mind was her ivy-covered home. Out the corner of her eye, Milli saw a portal snap open and shut, before another further down the way did the same. Her agonised brain could only think that one of the dragons was creating them so ran, pulling Makkan along with her. As they had almost reached the safety of the woodland area, a portal opened out right in front of them, cutting off their route. They were about to turn and run when Makkan recognised the men on the other side and shouted to them. In response to Makkan's shout, Eric and Milan ran through the portal. Eric didn't stop; he ran straight to Milli and, because of all the pent-up frustration, almost slapped her, burning with frustration for all the hurt and the loss which he had not even started to acknowledge. Milan stopped Eric with a side-step and the four stared at each other for a moment, breathing hard. Makkan broke the silence by telling them that Oroch had gone, that two other dragons had been sweeping the skies, but, judging from the expressions on the faces of Eric and Milan, it was obvious that they already knew what had happened.

'We have to get to Warwick. You are the only ones left who can stand up to the dragons, before you succumb and become our enemy.'

Eric grabbed Makkan's arm, demanded Milan conjure a portal, and not knowing what other action to take, the four returned to Warwick to a scene none of them had expected.

The castle area was surrounded by metallic holders. Each one was in their smart fitted suits, with their slick hairstyles and stern faces. Above the castle, an arc of dragons looked down on the growing number of people, their wings beating a rhythm that caught at eardrums like a shockwave and made the surrounding landscape pulsate, as if breathing. The air was crackling with the feeling of magic as both parties prepared for battle. Nobody had seen the four enter, but that soon changed as Makkan cried out. Looking down at her hand, she watched in horror as it began to transform; fingernails elongated into claws and scales rippled on the surface of her arms. She tried to grab at her shoulders as she could feel an immense pressure, but it was too late to warn anyone as the wings burst from her back, pushing the other three out of their way with the force. Her clawed hand went to her face as she felt the agony of teeth rearranging. The process seemed to be going in slow motion, but her cries caught the attention of the holders, and Prudence took her chance. Her hands rose and lightning seemed to crackle between her fingers. It lashed out toward Makkan and struck her on her wing, making her scream out in a half dragon cry and a human pained scream. Makkan swept her arms in a big circle and with the air power she created pushed Milan, Milli and Eric further away from her, giving her room to attack Prudence. The determination of her expression exposed her fangs as she half walked, half dragged herself towards the witch. What drove her nobody knew, but she blasted the holders with a cutting arc of air, sending them flying back into the growing crowd. Only Prudence stood her ground. The others gathered themselves together quickly, and all began to pull on their own magic to target the Air Walker. Hands were raised with lightning of assorted colours pulsing at their fingertips. They shot at her, but none hit her. At the point when all the holders released their power, seemingly out of nowhere, Oroch had landed on the ground and wrapped his wings about Makkan, his back taking the full power of the hit causing him to trumpet with the pain. His tail whipped out behind him, but his wings never moved from the protective cover they had created around his lover. The clouds began to churn, and the weather overhead turned dark. Oroch's power was turning to the negative as his great eyes looked at the injury that had been caused to Makkan. Blood dripped from her wing, and the scorched smell of flesh caught at anyone's throat who was near enough to smell it. Oroch lowered his head and delicately touched the top of her wing. Her transformation had been interrupted; she was neither human nor dragon but half of each, and it appeared that Prudence's aim had been better placed than anyone thought. Makkan's human hand raised up and tenderly touched the muzzle of the crystal sea blue dragon before going back to her side. A few drops of blood oozed through her fingers, and Oroch went into a rage. Milli stepped forward finally and, without thinking, spoke to Oroch.

'I will help her. Go.'

Milli placed a hand on Makkan's side and closed her eyes. The blue dragon must have felt the touch of the healer for he accepted her words and rose to join the ranks of beating wings in the sky.

The King's guards had formed ranks wherever they could, to protect the civilians of Warwick, but they were under orders to take no action yet. They held their shields and swords in shaking hands as they looked between the Governess of Coventry and the dragons in the sky. It was Prudence who broke the silence as she screamed at the dragons above.

'It is our turn to have the power. You had your time and you wasted it. You rotted in your caves and diminished into nothing. It is our time now. Magic has returned, and we hold the power now. We will rule this place and people will come to respect us, fear us or love us but you will not stand in our way.'

She gave some sort of order through her actions, and suddenly all the Coventry coven were unleashing their magic toward the dragons above.

Some of their aims hit their target. The cries of pain from the dragons were evidence enough. From that moment on, nobody knew which way to turn. Dragons swooped through the sky with trails of fire licking the land below them; sandstorms raged through the landscape, destroying anything they touched; rain was pelting the land as clouds swirled in ever darker circles. People were crying, witches were shouting and falling, and the smell of decay was everywhere. Nobody had ever seen Zyman use his skills before, and after this moment they would pray to never see them again. The plants, trees and vines all around them, snaked out to grab people that passed before retreating back into the earth and taking whoever they enveloped with them. With Milan frozen in fear and Milli tending to Makkan, it was only Eric who was seeing the full picture unfold before him. Suddenly facts finally registered in his mind and he shouted to his father.

'Call the guards back. Get them to take people to safety. The dragons are only attacking the holders. They are trying to fight around us!'.

This fact had snapped him into action, and he finally understood: he had it wrong. Running down from the gate he had one aim in his mind. His anger finally let loose and his time spent brawling payed off as he ran forward punching or kicking any holder that stood in his way.

Coventry and Birmingham were feeling the effects of the war raging in Warwick as storms seethed and the ground rocked with such force that the glistening metallic buildings started to crack. People looked about in confusion as systems of order failed with the wavering electricity supply.

Prudence was in the centre of the grounds and focused on the purple dragon that had swept a path before him with his bulk. She raised her hands to the air and, as words were whispered an orb grew in her hand. The focus was absolute, and when she unleashed the energy, it caught Lindany square on his back, and with an anguished cry he fell to the ground. He lay as still as stone, his eyes open, his body unmoving.

Milli was still trying to stem the blood from Makkan's wound, made all the more difficult because her mind could not work out what was dragon and what was human. The nerves and cells were like nothing she had worked with before. Her voice was calm, and all she could do was keep trying: managing to hold wounds together but unable to fix them.

Milan had finally come around from the shock of everything that had happened, and his eyes fell on Eric. He called out to his friend but there was no way he was going to hear him. The noise of battle was deafening. Seeing people running to intercept Eric from his path, Milan opened portals which the people fell through and disappeared. He continued to watch where Eric was going, from his vantage point by the gates, and, as his trick worked for a third time, he saw his friend raise his hand and give a thumbs up sign.

'So cocky' was all Milan said but he felt true pride in his friend right at that moment and continued to help as much as he could. On occasions he put portals in front of Eric for him to pass through, which meant he missed people running head on; other times he used his portals to cut people down who were part way through trying to strike with magic.

*The light and vibrations reached a crescendo and the DragonSoul Stone cracked - the jarring black crevice breaking its shell and shattering the stone into pieces. A soft sigh was emitted, and a slight wisp of mist formed for but a moment. The stone was now nothing more than a broken rock.*

The battle was reaching a crescendo with some dragons being unable to fly for the charred holes in their wings, or their blood slipping from beneath scales and tarnishing their colour. The warlocks and mages were reduced in numbers but still they fought. At that moment a piercing scream cut through all the noise like a knife through butter. The silence that followed was almost as though everything was on pause. Suddenly, there was a blast of magical energy that pulsed from a central point and rippled through everything it passed before dispersing around the edges, just like an expanding halo. Everyone looked to the epicentre of the blast to see Eric run a blade through Prudence's shoulder blades and out through her chest. As he had run the gauntlet of magical fire and explosions, with the aid of Milan's portals, he had reached for a guard's sword just as Prudence had made the final blow that had killed Lindany. As her hands had lowered from the blast and her eyes had stayed glued to the falling dragon, the momentum of Eric's run and the remnants of Prudence's magic had been her undoing. Eric moved the blade once more before the Governess dropped to the ground. For a moment nobody knew what to do. Everything was still, apart from the lapping breeze from the diminishing storm. The witches and warlocks looked to each other and, as they mustered their power once more, a voice seemed to enter every living being, pulling at their minds for complete attention.

<<*We are not enemies, you and I. We are creatures of magic who have suffered through power and greed. Magic of the land is for all, and is as natural as the air, but power corrupts, and your lord wanted all. You have all been fooled by her lies, you have all been twisted by her word. We dragons held our power for millennia to keep the peace between all beings of magic, but we failed. We diminished with our shame of not being able to prevent the many wars for power in our time. But magic dwindled and left the land as science and technology took over. It was only in our slumbering did we gain the wisdom to realise*

*that all could live together. But too much time had passed, and we were dying. We knew magic would return and those that sought its use for the corrupt would once again try and take it. So, we planned our path with humans. For this we are sorry, we misguided you all. Would you have accepted this role while knowing? Would you willingly have given your young to be consumed by our souls? We wish to protect. We wish to keep the balance of power and magic, and for this part we did not lie. Do not give your answers to this yet, but I now speak to you before me of the areas you call holds. Your leader was the corrupt, she controlled you as much as she tried to control all. Let this go and be at peace with the magic you have within you. Dragons, your life is your own. No more do you need to look to the balance, the power is within you now. I now let the mist take me whole and I leave you to your future>>*

A ripple of the dragon's outline was seen briefly, in a pose similar to when he had flown above Warwick, before it was dispersed into the air, its lifeforce gone from this world.

The words reverberated in people's minds, and all could see the confusion that was caused by the mist dragon's words. For a while, nobody moved; then, one by one, the holders began to disappear using the purple orbs as seen before in the board room. Eventually all but a handful remained. The dragons had all landed and formed an arc in front of the castle gates. The tone of their grumblings and keening sombre as Zyman had landed next to Lindany. He lowered his muzzle to touch him lightly on the forehead before opening his great maw and breathing over him. The negative energy of the Natural Walker washed over the fallen dragon, and soon his body decayed and turned to ash to follow the mist dragon on the wind.

The solemn scene was only broken when Makkan coughed. Milli still knelt beside her, but at that simple sound, Oroch was back beside her with a single flip of his wings and his tone almost an anxious purr as he looked from Milli to Makkan. Milli frowned for a long moment before she finally stood up and addressed the group of dragons and humans that had gathered around the gates.

‘My name is Milli. I am a holder from Coventry who came to the DragonSoul procession for my 18th Birthday. I am so sorry for...’ The remorse for the pain she had caused was plain to see in her mismatched eyes that nobody needed her to finish the sentence. She breathed hard for a moment before straightening her shoulders and looking about the group. ‘I did not have the teachings of the elders, nor have I ever been near the flow of energy that you call ‘the balance’. My dragon’s soul is called Yebby and we live in harmony inside me. I see now that it is different than how you have been living. Yebby and I can talk freely to each other, and so we have throughout all that has happened to us. The dragon that just spoke was the dragon of the mist; none of the dragons here can commune with you, and for that I am sorry, but I can hear their thoughts through Yebby. Not so for any of the other Walkers as your bonds have been formed with the balance and its transformations in mind.’ She looked then to the group seeking permission to continue. All encouraged her, and Oroch’s keening was hard to ignore.

Looking to Makkan and Milan, Milli smiled lightly. 'Both of you have been working with the balance, but less than the others. Makkan, your transformation into the majestic air dragon had begun, but the magic that hit you stopped your transformation. I was confused as to why I could not heal you, but Yebby has explained that you are between forms. You need to choose.'

The pain on the Air Walker's face was replaced by shock. Sweat broke out on her brow as she tried to think past the shaking of her shattered wing. Finally, she looked at Eric, the King and the others before turning to Oroch.

'I choose to be a dragon, to be with you.'

No sooner had she said the words, and her mouth had begun to form a 'goodbye', the transformation continued. It was as if the final decision had helped the healing process, and as her body twisted and morphed into the dragon, the new growth sealed wounds and healed membrane. With trumpets of joy, the beautiful silver white hide of Makkan was joined by Oroch in a dance which held their audience captive until they stopped and joined the ranks of dragons listening intently. Milan's thoughts made him smile as he wondered if John/Zyman had known that the love those two had, transcended both souls. Drawing his thoughts back to the moment, Milan coughed slightly and turned to Milli.

'What about me?'

Eyes glazed as Milli and Yebby conferred, then she turned to look at him apologetically.

'I am sorry, Milan; you are the same as me in that we did not continue to take the balance, but we used our powers willingly. Your DragonSoul knew this day was coming and has drifted into depression, feeling he could not complete his original mission to transform. You and I will not become dragons but will stay as we are. It is up to your dragon if he is willing to work with us in the form that he is and help communicate between dragons and the lands.'

Milan was not able to talk to his dragon in the same way that Milli was, and this was something he decided he would need to talk to her about. Not sure how to answer he nodded. 'I am willing. I will meditate tonight and seek the wisdom of Milan.' He quietly hoped his DragonSoul was listening.

As the speech had continued, Milli had been watching Eric. His eyes had not moved from the green dragon that was before him. His striking hair with his torn up three-piece suit and the water in his eyes would forever be etched on her mind. Slowly Zyman lowered his head and Eric placed a hand on the tip of his muzzle. Those still present were surprised that the dragon had allowed him to do this, but it was as if the dragon knew he needed his brother. Eric's hand stayed resting lightly as he turned to face Milli.

'Is my brother still in there? Are they now dragons with a human soul?'

Milli did not know how to answer, but Zyman grumbled lightly and closed his eyes. Milli nodded.

'They are there, but they are faint.'

That was all Eric needed to hear. He lifted his other hand to hold the dragon's snout for a moment before he stepped away.

'I will find a way.'

He turned and faced the people, 'You there, Council members of Coventry, Father, John. I decided before all of this took place that I would join the holds council and was accepted.' He turned then to slowly walk down the stairs. The King raised his arm and was about to call his son before Eric answered.

'I will take my place. I will grow within Coventry and see if I don't lead!' He turned back to the group and winked with the arrogance he always showed. 'Especially if I have a Walker by my side who can get me places.'

His grin and determination were infectious, and Milan nodded his acceptance with the first smile he had worn in a long while. Before Milli was able to think of anything to say, Eric turned to her, looked directly into her eyes and smiled. 'The dragons need you here. You are the bridge between our kinds and their wisdom will help rebuild this land. Make sure my brother, and the other human souls within, stay safe. Keep the balance. Keep the peace.' Milli nodded her agreement as the hum from the backdrop of dragons confirmed their acceptance.

Milan joined Eric and the last holders to remain. The Purple Walker opened a portal to Coventry, and all began to enter. Just as Eric stepped through the portal, he turned to look back at the wild image of Warwick castle and smiled.

'The year is 2167. Magic has returned to the land, and I will find a way brother.'

# The End

# New Generation Index

<u>Natural Walkers (Green DragonSoul)</u>

- Positive Energy: Nature, Growth
- Negative Power: Withering, Pestilence, Decay

**Milli** – Coventry – DragonSoul Yebby
John – Warwick – DragonSoul **Zyman**

<u>Water Walkers (Blue DragonSoul)</u>

- Positive Energy: Water, Sky, rain, mist
- Negative: Flooding, thunder, stagnation

Darryn – Exeter – DragonSoul **Oroch**
Andy – Exeter – DragonSoul Gilbran

<u>Air Walkers (Grey DragonSoul)</u>

- Positive Energy: Air, speed, windflow
- Negative: Storms, low pressures

Tanya – Truro – DragonSoul **Makkan**
Johan – Truro – DragonSoul Siska

<u>Fire Walkers (Red DragonSoul)</u>

- Positive: Fire, warmth, life
- Negative: Destruction, Elemental flames

Chris – Leeds – DragonSoul Ethany
Malinky – Leeds – DragonSoul Musany

Earth Walkers (Brown DragonSoul)

- Positive: Earth, Sand, building
- Negative: Storms, quakes, boulders

Joe – Cardiff – DragonSoul Tellany
Zack – Cardiff – DragonSoul Bechany

Ether Walkers (Purple DragonSoul)

- Positive & negative: Portals

Simon – Glasgow – DragonSoul **Milan**
Liam – Glasgow – DragonSoul **Lindany**

**Metallic Holds named in this book:**

Coventry
Plymouth
Manchester
Sheffield
Glasgow
Cardiff

**Natural Wilds named in this book:**

Warwick
Exeter
Truro
Leeds
Whole of Dorset

# About the Author.

Born in 1979, Sophia lives in south west Devon, with her cat. Sophia works alongside Dawn, with an excellent team of carers, at Teign Angels. Sophia also enjoys playing the fiddle in folk trio 'DevonBird'; and in a ceilidh band called the 'Mooncoin Barn Dance Band' This is Sophia's debut novel.

Thank you for joining me in this world.

Printed in Poland
by Amazon Fulfillment
Poland Sp. z o.o., Wrocław

57072170R00193